TEXAS RANGER CREEK IN

FULL CIRCLE

WESTERN ADVENTURES

SUNDOG SERIES 10

By

ASH LINGAM

&

DAVE WALTON

D1557104

a

TEXAS RANGER CREEK IN FULL CIRCLE

Copyright © 2018

By Ash Lingam & Dave Walton

All rights reserved.

ISBN: 13: 978-1723888717

Creative Commons No: 1809238460933

www.ashlingam.com

A Western Novel

b

TEXAS RANGER CREEK IN FULL CIRCLE

C

"No man in the wrong can stand up against a fellow that's in the right and keeps on a-comin'."

Captain Bill McDonald Texas Ranger

TEXAS RANGER CREEK IN FULL CIRCLE

This novel is dedicated to

Ernest Hemingway, who said:

All you do is sit down at a typewriter and bleed.

e

TEXAS RANGER CREEK IN FULL CIRCLE

f

OTHER NOVELS BY ASH LINGAM

THE BOUNTY HUNTERS SERIES

Bounty Hunters - Rancor Maleficent #1

Bounty Hunters – Roberto Rodriguez #2

Bounty Hunters – Mister Tom Horn #3

Bounty Hunters – Marshal Hoss Cole #4

THE SUNDOG SERIES

Sundog Comanche #1

Sundog Daze #2

West to Ranger Creek #3

Ranger Creek and the Gunslinger #4

Texas Ranger Creek's Old West Adventures #5

Texas Ranger Creek – West to Tombstone #6

Texas Ranger Creek & Tombstone's Bloody Bucket #7

Texas Ranger Creek & Cowboy Justice #8

Texas Ranger Creek in Range War #9

Texas Ranger Creek and Full Circle #10

RIDGE CREEK TRILOGY + ONE

Ragged Ridge Creek #1

The Battle of Lost Valley #2

Chisholm Trail to Deadwood #3

Lonesome Canyon #4

g

h

Table of Contents:

TEXAS RANGER CREEK IN FULL CIRCLE

j

CHAPTER 1:

EL PASO, TEXAS

Rowdy Bates, Tuc, Potak and I brought our horses up to a high lope as soon as we left the Comanche village. Us all intending to put as much distance between the danger and ourselves before the Comanche had a change of heart. What with me demanding our horses and walking off in the middle of a parley put the warriors off balance a bit and they turned their attention to the torturing of old man Bogardus. Starting with the removal of the foul nobleman's tongue. And ending the life of Will Bones. A man who murdered and did the bidding of the rich, but when it came time to die he cried like a baby and fouled himself. Much to the amusement of the Comanche Warriors as they watched the old woman practice her torturing skills on their captives.

"We were lucky that we left when we did," Tuc said with that wicked grin he makes. A gash of mouth with the edges turned up at the ends. "It is important for a man to know when it is time to leave. I figured that we would lose our scalps to the Comanche. I believe that they were scared of you, With Dead Eyes."

"They had no reason to kill us other than just being plain ornery as they called me to the parley, so proper protocol has to be followed by the Comanche as much as us," I replied, not having been really sure how they would react to my ordering our horses to be brought to us all sudden like.

"We must be the first two Tonkawa to ride out of a Comanche camp since they massacred our tribe along with the help of the Kiowa and Cheyenne. I never understood what the Plains Indians had against our people," Potak the Tonkawa Indian scout stated.

"Weston told me it was because you folks had the bad habit of feeding on some of your enemies upon occasion," Rowdy blurted out.

"That's no different from the customs of the Shoshoni or the Comanche when a Warrior Brave kills his first man in battle," Potak argued. "They eat their hearts and become a man and a respected warrior. Our customs have existed many hundreds of years. How long have your customs existed here in the wild country, With Dead Eyes?"

"I choose to ignore a man's personal business as long as he don't go waving it under my nose," I replied.

"I knew better than to wear my scalps into the Comanche camp," Tuc retorted. "I'm not stupid."

"You're a damn sight from stupid you crafty scoundrel," I snorted. "If you would spend more time working and less time trying to spy on everybody else's business it would be better appreciated."

"I do my job," the Tonkawa countered. "What I do with my own time is my affair."

It was late afternoon when Rowdy and I rode into El Paso and on to the Texas Ranger Post. Tuc and Potak had already disappeared the first chance they had, running off to who knows where to spread some more gossip most likely.

Most of the boys were sitting out on the porch listening to old Bill Vents tell another one of his yarns. The old gray-haired liar was drawing one and all into his spider web of tales of the Texas Rangers through the years. Sergeant Bill Vents must be the oldest Ranger in in the whole state. He seemed to be as old as the hills when I signed on years ago. Although he don't appear any older, it was hard to put a finger on his age, and he weren't giving up the information easy like.

Weston turned in his chair to face the courtyard and said, "Howdy Captain. It looks like you all made it there and back in one piece. But I don't see that old Scotsman Bogardus with you."

"Well, he wasn't worth the trade, Sergeant," I replied. "So we left him and Mister Bones to the tribe to deal with and that they did. His daughter was as happy as a pup with two tails there with the Comanche, so we left her with the warrior braves. I reckon that's the end of the range war with the Bogardus clan. I doubt that there be much left of the family from what I gather."

Just then I saw Marshal Dallas Stoudenmire heading for the porch, so Rowdy and I slid off of our mounts and tied Horse and Rowdy's cow-pony to the hitching rails just at the edge of the building. As the Marshal neared the group of men, I put my hand out to the reformed lawman.

"Good to see you made it, Ridge," Dallas said. "Y'all on your own?"

"Yep, just Rowdy and me," I replied. "The Tonkawa scouts ran off a spell before we got into town. Old man Bogardus is dead, as are all the gunmen he hired. Bertha Bogardus stayed with the Comanche, and a number of the folks that were employed on the Scotsman's wagon train snuck off while the Warrior Braves ransacked their wagons. We might want to send a few Rangers out to have a look for stragglers.

Make sure that they make it back to El Paso safely. I reckon they'll be strung out from here to the point of the conflict, which is a good spell on foot. According to their two scouts, Curley Bob Jones and Billy Behind the Duce there was another wagon with a passel of black folk and crackers who wandered off and headed down to Mexico to escape the old Scotsman. The old man tended to have his employees thrashed with a cat-o-nine-tails if they disappointed him. Something that seemed to be a relatively frequent occurrence."

"Things here in town are back to normal with my two Deputy Marshals Braggs and Hutch," Dallas replied. "Nobody has seen any more of those men in beige dusters. Slim even came into town while we were out visiting with the Comanche and said that they have not heard of any more ranch hands being bushwhacked, although they said that there is still a considerable amount of horse rustling going on. I figure that as we had our attention on the Bogardus clan for the last month or so the rest of the outlaws have begun to run a tad wild. Running down across the border and rustling cattle and horses from Pedro Mendez. I've also heard that many that venture down his way don't make it back."

"That Mexican has rustled as many horses and cattle north of the border as Texans have stolen from his stock down south of the Rio Grande. I figure that nobody knows whose cattle are whose by now. What with the brands all being doctored to look like another newly registered brand," I replied.

"I also heard that outlaw Lopez has been on the south side of the border in Paso del Norte. Right over the river. The Mexican law told me they saw him but didn't venture to attempt to apprehend the man. I reckon those boys didn't want to get captured and tortured or just shot on the spot."

I drew back my lips and spat through my teeth into the dust beside the porch and said, "That man sticks in my craw. I reckon it is time for me to deal with him once and for all."

"That is if you can find him," Dallas replied. "His is slipperier than a greased pig."

"That Mexican scoundrel Lopez usually finds us all on his own," Bill Vents stated. "Most of the time he grabs one of our boys while they're out tending to their personals."

"That ain't happened for some time now," Weston countered. "They go out three at a time nowadays. Ain't been another one captured since they go in a group. How do you figure to lure him out, Ridge?"

"I figure if he knows that I'm after him he won't be able to resist having a look for me. He wants to kill me as much as I want to kill him."

"If he's close, it's time to go after him," Weston added. "If not, he will ride south again to his hideout a few days into Mexico then nobody is going to find him."

"We just got done fighting off outlaws in a range war," Clinton Westwood complained. "A man has a right to take a rest for a few days, don't he? The Sergeants made us stay cooped up here in the Ranger post for the whole time you were out meeting with the Comanche."

"That was because if the Captain needed us quick like we would all be easy to find and could head out in short notice," Bill explained. "But, I must agree with Clinton. It has been a good spell since we have had any time off, boss."

"Well, alright then. Let me get cleaned up and I'll tag along with the Sergeants," I ordered. "The rest of you can take off now if you want. You coming with us Dallas?"

"Sure," the Marshal replied. "We can head over to Rosa's Cantina for some refreshments."

"I'll be having some horizontal refreshments with my whiskey," Sergeant Winston Smith added as he displayed a grin from one ear to the other.

"Sit down, and I'll fix you up a cup of coffee, Marshal Stoudenmire," Humphrey Willow offered. "I still got a few pieces of pie left too. I hid it from the boys for when the Captain got back."

"That was mighty big of you Ranger Willow," I replied, the Texas Ranger knowing I have a notorious sweet tooth and all.

Dallas and I joined the two Sergeants on the porch as the other boys grabbed their hats and pistols and headed on into town. Everyone but Humphrey who generally tagged along with Weston, Bill and me. Ranger Willow was a reliable man even with him having only the one arm. I have never heard him complain about the loss once since the outlaw Lopez lured that bear into our camp and cut Humphrey's left arm clean off just a few inches below the elbow. One swipe of his massive paw and the claw cut through flesh and bone like it was butter. Plus as he was a mite older than the Ranger pups, he had little need for the acting up that the young men tend to do.

"Here you go," Humphrey said as he sat the tray down and passed the plates to each of the men along with a fork. "If you want cinnamon just hold your tin plate out, gentlemen."

The four men sat there and enjoyed the fresh apple pie. Making it seem like everything was back to normal. At least as normal as can get with me being transferred to El Paso. Well, it could be worse. They could have had me head for Austin and sit at a desk for a spell. I must admit that the way things were seen from Austin and how I saw them here, were often a conflict of opinions.

"I don't ever seem to see eye to eye with the bosses at the Texas Ranger office in Austin," I said to my old friends sitting there on the porch. "In the past, I have often ignored orders and done as I've seen fit. Even back when our

Captain was John RIP Ford. I guess we best be thankful we ain't getting all the government we're paying for."

"Just the fact that they sent us to rescue that old Scottish Bogardus sumbitch is clear proof that they don't know their assholes from their earholes," Bill Vents replied. "I half expected you to return with that vile old man. I think you should have told Austin that you went and couldn't find him and just stayed right here in El Paso. Why risk your life for nothing."

"You ain't going to make me go back to Laredo with Rowdy, are you Captain?" Henry Willow asked all nervous like. "I've been serving under you for a long time, Sir. It would sit with me might poorly if I had to move on. Who would you have to cook for you if you send me with the boys?"

"Rest easy Ranger Willow," I replied with a smile. "You ain't going nowhere, Pard. Who would make my pie and baked apples? Somebody has to keep an eye on the two Sergeants and me."

"Who else will be staying here with us Ridge?" Weston asked.

"Toby Bees for sure, along with Humphrey here. Clinton Westwood, Ace McCoy and Billy Joe James we need here too, so I guess I'll just be sending Rowdy and Travis Picket back. We'll send Tuc and Potak along with them to make sure they don't get into any trouble and arrive safely."

"And who is going to keep Tuc out of trouble?" Weston snickered. "I ain't heard you threatening to shoot them of late, boss."

"I really never intended to shoot either of those two," I replied. "They ain't all that bad if you can keep them pointed in the right direction. Anyway, when have you ever seen me threaten to shoot someone and not do so? Other than Tuc that is. Just goes to show you it was my way of getting them to do what I wanted."

"I'm ready for some cold beer," Bill said as he unfolded his short but stout frame from his seat and kicked Weston's chair. "Let's get going. It's already dark and I ain't had a drink yet."

Humphrey headed into the kitchen and came back out with his scatter-gun in the crook of his stump. And we all four walked down the main street of town heading towards Rosa's Cantina.

As we walked toward the saloon we moved past the Ernesto Zapata General Store and out there, standing in the front door was the most beautiful woman I have ever seen in my entire life. I couldn't take my eyes off of the lady, such was her captivating eyes. Then she looked right at me and smiled, flashing perfect white teeth, and a twinkle sparkled in her eye.

"Look out, Ridge!" Weston shouted as I walked right into a pig that was standing in the middle of the road and fell flat on my face.

I pushed my mug up and out of the street, and I managed to get my knees and onto my feet again as I dusted off the dirt from my clothing. I could clearly hear the hearty deep laugh of the woman on the porch. She was so tickled she stood there with her hands on her hips and arched her back as she laughed.

"It wasn't all that funny," I said in a slightly aggravated voice just loud enough for her to hear.

"Oh but I am afraid that it was indeed that funny, sir," the woman said in a brave voice. "There are few things more entertaining than a man making a fool of himself while being hypnotized by a beautiful woman."

"You certainly think a lot of yourself, don't you ma-am?" I replied now getting more aggravated by the woman, even though I couldn't seem to take my eyes off of her.

"My name is Miss Lola Zapata Gonzalez," she said as she stepped down off of the General Store porch with her hand reaching out for mine.

I just stood there totally lost for words. I tried like the dickens, but I couldn't come up with a thing to say.

"You do know how to talk, don't you Mister Texas Ranger?" Lola asked as she continued to giggle. "Why, you scratched your forehead when you fell. Come on along with me to my father's store, and I'll clean it and put some alcohol on it. You three mosey on along to wherever it was you were heading. I will be taking care of your Ranger friend here."

"The name is Ridge, ma-am," I finally blurted out.

It was all Weston, Bill and Humphrey could do to keep from laughing, which would have made things even worse. But as ordered by Miss Zapata they moved on out towards the saloon. And Lola grabbed my hand and practically drug me over to the store and inside where she sat me down and told me not to move. Shortly returning with some bandages, alcohol, and merbromin.

"It really isn't anything, ma-am," I said to Miss Zapata. "No need to go to such a fuss."

"Now, sit still and stop objecting. With the way you were looking at me you would think that my giving you such attention would be exactly what you would want. Am I right or not?"

I don't think that I have ever been so lost for words in my life. I have never been a forward man with women. Unless they were working girls and even then, I never acted like Weston Smith. All smooth like and always knowing what to say. Now I find myself content with just sitting here with Lola dabbing the orange antiseptic onto my forehead.

"I believe that you'll live, Mister Ridge."

"Hola, Lola. ¿Pasa algo aqui?" a well-dressed older Mexican gentleman asked as he walked over to where I sat. "Is everything alright?"

"Don't worry Papá. This is Mister Ridge, a Texas Ranger," Lola explained. "He stumbled over a pig in the street, and I brought him here to tend to his bruise."

"Excuse me, Sir. I am Captain Ridge Creek of the Laredo Texas Rangers. I have just been transferred here until further orders. I ain't intending to be a bother."

"I have been trying to get you to talk since you first looked at me. And now you go and tell my father your life story," Lola said with a chuckle. "So I have found myself a Texan Captain. It must be my lucky day."

"Now mind yourself, Lola," her father warned her. "If you don't behave I will send you back to my other store on the south side of the border. Be careful with Lola, Captain. I believe that you will find she is a handful and then some."

CHAPTER 2:

THE OUTLAW LOPEZ

Lopez sat cross-legged before the roaring fire. Here in Mexico, he felt confident that his reputation would deter anyone from considering turning him into the law. They knew he would just kill the lawman and then he would kill them, their children, their parents, and their friends. This nefarious Mexican bandit was like that. He reeked insidious revenge on those that went against him. So the poor Mexican peasants never even considered crossing him.

The flames flickered across the half-breed's face. The mask of a torturous villain. He was half Indian and half Mexican and one-hundred percent murderous. His long hair and drooping mustache were greasy and stuck to his head and face with sweat. But the sweltering heat from the fire didn't bother a man such as Lopez. He preferred the hard ways. Living in the wilds. Fighting and taking what he wanted. Never allowing himself to get soft. As he sat there on a horse blanket, he stared into the fire as if searching for some sign. Some sort of vision.

There was considerable movement in the outlaw's campsite. About a dozen men went about cleaning weapons and tending to their rigs. Another half dozen Mexican women tended to washing the clothing and to fixing the meals. Two scrawny dogs were barking at the edge of the fire where the women cooked. Occasionally Lopez would pick up a stone and hurl it at the canines. Temporarily running the mutts off, although they would eventually return and begin to bark again. Hoping to get some of the dinner scraps.

As the outlaw sat silently before the flames, a Comanche rode into his camp. The Warrior Brave was immediately surrounded by Lopez's men with their long-rifles in hand.

"Let him be," Lopez ordered. "He's my Comanche spy. We can't kill him, or we won't be getting any more information from the man."

The Comanche spy was named Ho-Tu. He worked at one time or another for the Comanche, Tonkawa, Kiowa, Cheyenne, Texas Rangers, Army, and of course Lopez. A man with free travel rights just due to the fact that he can acquire relevant information and provide the same to his clients or also valuable information that any of his contacts might want to send to their enemies, depending who is doing the asking and how much they were paying. The man with the painted face was a trader of sorts. Trading gossip, information and at times misinformation for cash money. Ho-Tu's face was a mask giving away no sign of his emotions nor did he seem to have any fear whatsoever. Especially while visiting with the infamous murdering scoundrel that Lopez was.

Lopez was not usually a man to respect a truce or a parley. Often killing the folks, he arranged to meet with. But he had been working with this old spy for years as had many. Killing this man would undoubtedly bring repercussions to the Mexican outlaw. So Lopez was on his best behavior as the Comanche took his place, sitting cross-legged by the hot fire alongside the Mexican bandit.

"The heat is good," Ho-Tu stated. "Sweat removes the body's toxins and the evil spirits that poison your body."

The Comanche was a big man by Indian standards. Over six feet tall and all lean muscle. He carried a Winchester rifle, two Colt revolvers, a tomahawk and a long knife he kept in a sheath in his moccasin boot. Lopez looked the man up and down. Looking for some hint of expression or body language indicating what this dangerous Indian wanted.

"Thanks for being the go-between to buy two of the folks from the Scotsman's wagon train," Lopez told Ho-Tu. "I have them tied up waiting for whatever surprise I can think up for them. I haven't paid you for our last business. How much do I owe you?"

"The wagon train people was a small thing. You could have captured a couple of them all on your own if you rode north of the border. They were there for the taking. I figure that there are still some strays if you wish for me to acquire one or two more. But the information that I have for you is of much more value than a few settlers, although it will be expensive," Ho-Tu warned.

"How will I know if the information is worth the money if you don't tell me what it is first?" Lopez said with a crafty smile.

"You know my reputation" the Comanche replied with an expressionless face. "It is beyond reproach. What I say is always true. That is why I am still alive and can trade in gossip and concrete information while traveling freely between the tribes and the white men. And of course to come here and feed you information. What I have to tell you will be important enough for you to forget about torturing such worthless people as settlers traveling west. Not much of a challenge for anyone that lives on the Great Plains."

"How much and exactly what do you want in exchange for this particular piece of information?" Lopez asked the Comanche in Spanish, being the common language down here on the Mexican border.

Lopez spoke Comanche, but he vowed never to speak the language again when he was banished from his mother's tribe as a young boy. That's when Lopez's father demanded that he be trained in the ways of the rustler, thief, and killer just like his outlaw parent. He had already learned all that was of importance to the Comanche. Everything but respect to most other human beings, which Lopez felt was a waste of time.

"Ten Winchester rifles," Ho-Tu replied. "And five hundred rounds of ammunition."

Lopez whistled and said, "That is a mighty high order you've just made. What in the world do you have that is worth so much? How about I give you gold and silver instead of the long-rifles?"

"No, the long-rifles are wanted by Mukwooru, the Comanche Spirit Talker. He asked With Dead Eyes to make the same trade for the old Scottish man, but Captain Creek left him to die at the hands of the old Comanche woman."

Lopez immediately sat up as straight as an arrow at the mention of his lifelong enemy, Captain Ridge Creek of the Texas Rangers. Or With Dead Eyes to the Comanche and Kiowa.

"What does With Dead Eyes have to do with your gossip, Ho-Tu?" Lopez flashed angrily.

"First you must agree to give me the rifles," the Comanche replied.

"You'll have your guns and the five hundred rounds of flathead .44 cartridges," Lopez stated with the wave of his hand as if the request is nothing. "So what is it you have to say? Spit it out now as I am running out of patience."

The Mexican outlaw now focused his evil eyes on the Indian. Now no more than two fine slits as he stared at the Comanche Warrior, waiting for the vital information that he had brought here to the outlaw camp.

"With Dead Eyes is coming to kill you," the spy-related. "He will ignore the illegalities of entering Mexico. Creek intends to come after you with a dozen Texas Rangers, and most of them are said to be battle hardened veterans. He has been transferred to El Paso permanently."

The information made a noticeable change in Lopez's disposition. He was now very friendly to the spy. Grinning like a weasel in a hen house.

"Come with me to see to the captives," Lopez offered. "If you wish I'll give you one of them to torture yourself. I now have more important matters to deal with than two scruffy settlers from Europe."

As the outlaw and the Comanche walked over to the other side of the Mexican camp, they saw two men dressed in the clothing of a poor immigrant. Clod hopper boots with wool pants and shirt. Both wore a rope as a belt to hold the men's britches up. Both Scotts were standing back to back, each tied to a wooden post. A rope around their feet and another around their waists. Then they had wet rawhide pig stringing tied around their neck. As the leather dried, it shrunk, slowly cutting off more and more oxygen from the captives.

"Would you like to kill one of them Ho-Tu?" Lopez offered.

"I am in a hurry, and it would take too long," he replied. "They are already so scared that they have soiled themselves. I prefer to torture brave warriors over poor white people who are not worth wasting an arrow or time on."

Lopez took the remark as a slight to himself. He never did like Ho-Tu, but he knew he was valuable to the tribes and whites. If he killed him or tied him to a stake, he would soon have half of the Warrior Braves from three tribes after him. Instead, he grabbed a stool and took it over to the first white man.

Lopez was a terrible villain, but he was sort of short. So he used the stool to reach up high enough that he could have easy access to the Scotsman's head. He then took the spoon he had in his hand and scooped out first one eye and then the other as the victim screamed. The second Scottish immigrant began to cry too, although he couldn't see what had been done to his friend from their faraway motherland.

Lopez took the two eyes, one in each hand, between his thumb and index finger and held them up to his own and walked around to the second man tied to the stake.

"Now I have four eyes with which to see, Amigo," he screamed cackling like a hyena. "When I have yours I will have six eyes to see with."

The second man continued to scream as he used the spoon to remove his two eyes as well. Scooping them out like they were pieces of watermelon. Leaving the two men in their own world of pain. Left to look into the spirit world with eyeless sockets. Dark, bloody holes now appeared in the men's faces where their eyes had been minutes before.

"I am leaving," Ho-Tu said as he turned to head out. "It's too noisy here. Make sure that you get my rifles to me, Lopez."

Spited again, Lopez became impatient with the two captives and cut their throats to shut them up. Silence immediately returned to the camp.

Only the sounds of the tin pots and pans now remained as the Mexican women prepared the meal. No-one in the camp giving the tortured captives any mind.

CHAPTER 3:

STRAGGLERS

Toby Bees and Rowdy Bates rode out of El Paso in the direction of the battle with old Lord Bogardus and the men hired by Allan Pinkerton and the Comanche Warriors. It was the morning after Captain Creek and Rowdy had returned from the Comanche camp. Both young men were now riding with their eyes peeled for signs of any dangerous elements, although things had seemed to have settled down considerably. The

Comanche were temporarily appeased with the spoils they had captured in the attack of the wagon-train. The men hired by the Chicago detective agency were all dead along with the Scotsman himself.

"I can't believe that the Captain sent me to clean up the mess after the battle with the Bogardus men and the Comanche" Rowdy Bates complained. "I don't mind looking for the stragglers' none, but I always have to deal with the dead folks. I'm going to be a Captain for Pete sakes, Toby."

"You ain't more than a Sergeant until you get back to Laredo, so you best do as the Captain says and stop your complaining. I've got left with the same task as you and I ain't going on and on about it. I reckon the faster we get at the chore, the sooner we'll be done."

Rowdy and Toby each pulled a string of saddled horses for any survivors that they might encounter. That and a pick with two shovels to tidy up the dead. Captain Creek told them to bury the innocent folks in separate graves and the gunmen and their bosses in a common grave.   They didn't intend to give any more special treatment to the Bogardus family.

The two young Texas Rangers had ridden out early so they made good time and it wasn't long before they found the first stragglers. It was a man who looked like death himself. Tall all dressed in black with his eyes sunken back in his head making shadows over them. He was accompanied by his young son dressed exactly like the father.

"Y'all with the folks running from the wagon train?" Toby Bees asked the two.

"My name is Mister H. Rath, and this is my son Obadiah Rath. We were servants of the Scottish Lord Bogardus. I tended to his executions," the man said as the Lunger began to have long coughing jags bringing up copious amounts of mucus. "Excuse me gentlemen, but I am apparently also in need of a physician."

"You sure don't sound too healthy, Mister Rath," Toby replied. "You and your boy grab yourselves two horses from the string I got trailing me. We will ride on back to where the battle was and check for other survivors."

"Oh, I don't wish to return to such a ghastly sight, sir," Rath replied with conviction.

"It is not a question or an option, Mister Rath," Rowdy informed the man. "We were sent to tend to the safety of the survivors and to bury the dead and we ain't leaving you nor our horses out of our sights. We have our own orders; sir and I have no intention of eschewing from them. The Captain don't take kindly to poorly executed patrols. So if you want to continue on towards El Paso on your own and on foot that is your own decision. But if you are to ride one of our horses and go with us so we can protect you, it will be only if you follow our orders."

"I don't feel up to walking anymore Mister Rath," the man's son, Obadiah said. "What if the Indians show up again?"

"There is safety in numbers out here in the wild country, Mister," Toby Bees added. "You best do as Ranger Bates says and go along with us. We don't intend to stay out here any more time than is necessary."

Allan Pinkerton of Chicago

The two Scotsmen mounted a couple of the horses and continued on towards the wagon-train with the pair of young Rangers. As they moved forward, they picked up a total of eleven survivors. Mostly walking alone except for a man and wife. The only woman they found alive or not captured. At least eleven folks were still healthy enough to walk this far and not die. A couple of them had some wounds suffered by the Comanche but nothing that they would not recover from.

When the thirteen riders finally made it to the battleground things were strewn about for a half a mile. Many of the folks who traveled with old man Bogardus had perished at the hands of the Comanche. Others from the explosion that was set out to kill the gunmen hired by Allan Pinkerton at the bequest of Lord Bogardus.

"This looks like something out of the Bible," Toby whispered as the rode up. "I reckon death pays all debts."

"Let's not waste time and get the graves dug," Rowdy whispered as he looked around himself at the carnage.

"Six feet of dirt makes us all equal," Mister Rath observed. "Death is the wish of some, relief of many, and the end of all."

The bodies closest to the sock bombs were torn to bits. The farther away from the epicenter of the blast, the better shape the bodies were in. But it was one hell of a gruesome task, to say the least. The dead on the far end of the wagon-train were killed by the Comanche, mostly with arrows or spears. When the Indians have the upper hand, they usually don't waste bullets on folks that can easily be killed with the weapons of their ancestors. Usually a Warrior Brave's weapons of choice, it being the braver way to fight. Anybody can kill with a pistol or rifle. A brave Warrior will close in on the intruder and kill him with a well-placed arrow or capture them and torture them slowly.

"We should have brought a couple of rakes for the gun hands," Rowdy stated. "Most of them are pretty much scattered all over from the nails in the sock-bombs. Where did the Captain ever think up such a thing? The sock bombs and all. Did you see how the hot axle grease stuck to the Bogardus gun hands? Never seen anything like it."

"When Captain Creek gets a bee in his bonnet it's usually a good idea," Toby Bees replied. "It rendered a dangerous situation for all of us to nothing at all. We didn't fire one shot if I recall correctly. What the sticky bombs didn't take care of the Comanche did."

So the two men dug for a while and then one by one the Bogardus employees' grabbed shovels from what was left of the wagon-train and helped dig the graves. Each and every one of them was intent on getting some distance between them and this place of utter destruction. Some wagons were reduced to kindling with an odd intact wheel here or there. But most everything for a few hundred feet was blown to pieces.

It was nearly nightfall when the twelve men and one woman were back in their saddles and heading away from the carnage.

"Why don't we stop here for the night and sleep before we ride five or six hours back to El Paso, Rowdy?" Toby Bees asked.

"I ain't staying out here with all those ghosts roaming about," Sergeant Bates replied emphatically. "I ain't no fool. Its bad luck to linger about with the freshly buried."

"One of these days that superstitious streak you have is going to be the end of you, Ranger Bates," his friend retorted.

"No sir, one of these days my wisdom on good and bad luck is going to save me as it has probably done in the past," Rowdy replied. "How do you know that my bad luck precautions haven't saved us a bunch of times already?"

"Because every time we get in a bad spot, the Captain gets us out of it. So it ain't got nothing to do with good or bad luck. It has to do with common sense and Ridge Creek being smart."

"Ain't that Tuc and Potak sitting under that scraggly tree out there ahead of us?" Rowdy Bates asked.

"It's getting too dark for me to tell. You know you have better eyesight than I do," Toby replied.

But sure enough, as dusk came, they rode up to the two Tonkawa scouts sitting under the only tree in sight. Crossed legged as mute as two stumps.

"Howdy Tuc, Potak," Toby Bees said happy to see his two friends. "What are you two doing out here?"

"We followed you both to the site of the skirmish to make sure no Comanche returned," Tuc replied. "We just came to look after you, Toby."

"Why that is mighty kind of you both, but I figure that Rowdy and I can take care of ourselves just fine," Sergeant Bees replied.

"There is no sense taking chances that ain't necessary," Potak added. "You boys are riding your horses too hard. The spirits of white men can't hurt you out here. But you bake those horses, and they won't be worth shite if we have to run for it."

"Rowdy is nervous staying around here with all those dead folks, so we were pushing our mounts to get some distance."

"Rowdy is too worried about dying," Tuc said.

"I'm not afraid of death," Bates replied. "I just don't want to be there when it happens."

"You're worrying about nothing," Toby retorted.

"Death is often a distant rumor to the young," Potak stated. "It is a law and not a punishment. It is best to respect death and ride on the safe side whenever possible."

"Didn't I tell you?" Rowdy Bates countered. "Being smart and being superstitious is pretty much the same thing."

CHAPTER 4:

WINDY RIDGE RANCH

When Slim Pickens from the Double HH Ranch and Fred Banks from the Soggy Bottom spread rode up to the Ranger Post, I was a bit surprised. I hadn't heard of any more trouble from the ranches or the cowboys, and these two men didn't exactly strike me as the visiting types.

Both men had heavy loads in keeping the ranches working correctly and the ranch hands in line. I had been sitting on the Ranger post porch nursing a cheroot in my white chair when the pair rode up. I stretched out my six-foot-two-inch frame and walked out to the hitching rails to see what the trouble was.

"Howdy, Ridge," Slim Pickens said straight off with a grin while Fred Banks from the Soggy Bottom tipped his hat. "Glad to see that you're still alive. From what I heard you put the powder to those Bogardus gun hands. Is it true you made some kind of sticky-bombs out of socks and nails?"

"I never gave them a name as it was just something that I thought up at the last minute," I replied. "But the names sounds pretty much like what it was. Flying nails and axle grease covered in kerosene. Stuck to everything like it was glue burning right through clothing and all. So what kind of problems do we have now? I know you two ain't here to shoot the breeze, are you?"

"Actually we couldn't be better," Slim replied. "And we ain't here for no assistance either. We came here to repay you for all the help you bestowed upon us."

"I was just doing my job, gentlemen," I replied. "Step down off of your horses, and I'll have Humphrey make up a bit of coffee. Ranger Willow! Come on out here and bring some more coffee and two more cups."

The ranchers took a seat, and both of them sat there silent. Something common for such men but both men had shit-eating grins on their faces, which wasn't normal as far as I've seen of Slim and Fred in the past.

Humphrey didn't take but a few minutes and he came out with a fresh pot of Texas coffee and a half dozen frying pan biscuits with butter and honey.

"Here you go, gentlemen," Willow said as he passed the biscuits around. "It's not good to drink strong coffee on an empty stomach."

The four of us sat there on the porch until we had finished the last bite of biscuit and the last of our coffees. At first, I figured that Slim had some bad news for me, which is usually the case when someone hunts down the Captain of the

Texas Rangers. But they both seemed to be in too good a mood for folks who have bad tidings to bestow on a man. I waited quietly for them to get to the why and what of their visit. Being a patient man, in general, I started to fish around in my vest pocket to grab a cheroot.

"I have just what you want Captain," Slim Pickens said with a grin on his mug as he passed me a cigar. "I bought these at the Zapata General Store. That pretty young lady there told me they are from South America or some such place. She swore that they were better than the cheap smokes that we all usually enjoy."

Each one of us lit up a fancy cigar from who knows where and we continued the silence. I must admit it wears me out some waiting on the Cowboys to get around to what they consider proper manners before picking at the bone. So finally I tired of all the hee-hawing and stood to my feet.

"Well boys, I know you ain't here to drink coffee, eat biscuits or smoke cigars, so what is it that y'all need?" I asked the two ramrods.

"I thought you'd never ask," Slim replied with a chuckle. "During our little range war, five ranches were abandoned. Mostly the ones close to the border with Mexico. The owners ran off when they thought that Bogardus would come to their home and wipe them out. So they sold us their cattle and extra horses and packed up their things and moved on. Most of them towards California looking for greener pastures. A couple of them managed to sell their places to neighboring ranches, but two of them were just left vacant. They were totally abandoned."

"And what does that have to do with me, Slim?" I asked.

"Well Fred and me here along with the boys at the T-Bone ranch arranged to have the rights to these two ranches. One of them is called the Windy Ridge Ranch. I couldn't help but think of you Ridge. So we had the ranch put into your name. We figure that it don't cost nobody a dime and you deserve something for saving our spreads other than a thank you. So, if you fancy it, you're now the owner of a ranch near the border with Mexico, but still here in Texas. It ain't a big spread like the Double HH or the Soggy Bottom, but it's a good start. There is a fine ranch house, barn, and a sturdy corral. It comes along with two hundred acres of land."

"Y'all are joshing me, right?" I replied.

"Do we strike you like the type of men to josh about such a thing?" Fred asked me. "Or much of anything for that matter."

"No, as a matter of fact, you don't," I answered. "I don't reckon there are any rules in the Texas Rangers that say that I can't own my own place."

"Well this here is the deed," Slim said as he passed a thick envelope with the documents to the Windy Ridge Ranch inside. "You are now officially a rancher."

"How about you bring out that bottle of the good whiskey in my desk drawer, Humphrey," I said. "This deserves a little celebrating."

"Yes Sir," Ranger Willow replied as he ran off to grab the bottle of spirits.

The two ranch bosses outlined the whereabouts of the spread and decided that they would spend the night in El Paso and tomorrow morning we would ride out to have our first look at my property. My own ranch. That did sound pretty damned good now, didn't it? Weston Smith, Humphrey Willow and Bill Vents all rode out with us. We got an early start and were already out of town when we saw the first hint of light begin to show on the horizon. Slowly growing to a brighter orange until the fiery sun stood there in the sky on the edge of the world. The summer heat was already noticeable on the skin, quickly eliminating the early morning coolness brought from the mountains.

"So how far a ride is it to our new ranch," Sergeant Smith asked.

"Our ranch?" I asked, surprised. "I didn't hear your name when Fred and Slim mentioned the land and the ranch house."

"It's only fair, Captain," Bill Vents added. "We did a lot of the work and Weston, and I rode all the way over here to help you out. How are you going to run a ranch on your own anyway? What with your Rangering job and all."

"I worked as a cowboy all my youth before I joined the Texas Rangers," Weston Smith added. "I figure that you'll need us both if you want to have a go at it actually working. If you ain't planning to do anything with the Windy Ridge

Ranch, then you best just pass on it as it would be going to waste."

"You do have a point, Pard," I replied as I pondered on what Bill and Weston said. "Actually, I never have considered owning my own place until Slim and Fred here offered it. I really don't know how to even go about starting things up. I've been a Texas Ranger since I was sixteen and tended to and swept up a general store before that. I really don't know much of anything except for chasing down outlaws and fighting Comanche and Kiowa."

We all rode on in silence. Getting closer to the Windy Ridge Ranch with every step. We traveled on for more than half the day and finally came to the top of a summit. Down in the valley was a medium-sized ranch house in the shape of an L. It wasn't in the best repair and could use some whitewash, but it looked water tight and sturdy enough. There was a good size corral right next to the barn. The barn had a hole in the roof that you could drive a small herd of cattle through, but other than that the spread looked fine indeed.

"Is there any water?" I asked the ramrods.

"There was an old dry creek bed down behind the house," Fred Banks said. "When old John Benet moved in here we made two dams in the freshwater springs by the lake up on my spread and directed water to fill his creek. So you have all the water you need. Most of the bigger spreads here share the water with the neighbors no matter how far-flung they are. There is a well over to the left side of the building where water is stored in the case the creek bed dries up in the summer."

"It sure does look like a nice home," Humphrey Willow said in nearly a whisper.

"And I'll be expecting you to do our cooking as long as we are there, Ranger Willow," I said to the man who had been as steady as a stone his entire time serving under me.

"Well let's ride on down and check it out," Bill Vents said as he put a spur to his horse and headed out at a quick lope. All of us started our way down the hill chasing after old Bill. As we got closer, I saw two men sitting cross-legged on the porch. Fred and Slim immediately pulled up and drew their Winchesters from their sheaths and levered a round into the chamber of each gun."

"Put the guns away boys," I said with a snicker. "Those are my two Tonkawa scouts. They always show up wherever it is I'm going sort of unannounced. I would have been surprised if they hadn't popped up all sudden like."

All six of us rode toward the house, right under a wooden sign with the words Windy Ridge Ranch painted on it in red letters. Then across the way up to the ranch house. I slid off of Horse and tied him to the hitching post.

"What are you two doing here?" I asked Tuc and Potak.

"We came to see the Ranger's new ranch," Potak replied.

"Why, how could you have known about us giving the Captain a ranch?" Slim asked with surprise on his face.

"Indian gossip," Potak replied. "White men talk too much to keep secrets, so the gossip travels quickly."

"Its true gentlemen," Bill Vents said to Slim and Fred. "Ain't no way to get news faster than with Indian gossip. Best way to get information out too. Works both ways."

"I like the porch," Tuc said as he stared hard at the two ramrods.

"Don't mind Tuc, there," Weston said. "He ain't friendly to us most of the time."

"It don't look like you're going to have much trouble populating this ranch, Captain," Slim snickered.

"Too bad about the roof on the barn," Fred added. "A twister ran through here a couple of weeks ago and must have skipped right over the top of the building and just hit the center. There you already have something for all these helpers to do."

When we walked into the ranch house building, it was clear that it had been ransacked. Most of the pots, pans, and whatnot had been taken along with part of the sparse furniture. The table was still there, but only one chair remained. It was painted white.

"It does look like this is the place," I said when I laid my eyes on the white chair.

"Looks like the Comanche had been snooping around to see what was left," Fred added.

"Is that what the gun-slats are for on the shutters?" Weston asked.

"They were installed a couple of years ago, but the Comanche have been raiding south of the border of late. The ranches around here are too well armed, and there are lots of cowboys. It's easier pickings in Mexico," Slim replied.

"Too many Winchesters," Tuc said. "The Comanche have old weapons and are no match for the repeater long-rifles."

"Fred and I better be heading out towards home, or we won't get there before dark," Slim said. "Enjoy your new home, Ridge. You earned it."

I shook the two men's hands and watched as they mounted up and rode out and under the sign that said Windy Ridge Ranch.

"We best be heading back too, boys," I said to the three Rangers.

"Who is going to look after the ranch, Captain?" Humphrey Willow asked.

"Tuc and Potak are here," I replied with a chuckle. "I doubt much happens if these two characters are around. Tomorrow we can buy provisions and a few more chairs and some kitchen supplies. The day after tomorrow I figure that Bill and Humphrey here should take a buckboard wagon and supply the ranch house a bit. Weston and I will be out in a few days."

We made it back to El Paso about an hour after dark without incident. We were all tired from riding all day. So we tended to the horses and hit the hay.

The next morning I was up at four o'clock and had an early ride around the outskirts of town. I didn't expect any problems and wasn't looking for anything in particular, but I did need a spell to get my head around the idea of owning a home of my own. Well, at least pretty much my own. My name was on the deed and all. And not a week ago I met Lola, and she makes me so damned confused that I can't have a conversation with her without putting my foot in my mouth. All she does is make fun of me, but since she let me steal that one kiss, I can't get her off my mind. Seems like things are pushing me to consider settling down.

I rode back into the Ranger Post at just after sunrise and Humphrey was standing on the porch with a hot kettle of coffee and some frying pan biscuits and gravy on a tray.

"Step down and have a seat, Captain," Ranger Willow said. "You go ahead and eat, and I'll tend to your horse."

"That is mighty big of you," I replied as I sat down on my white chair and dug into the biscuits."

All this thinking about settling down was making me hungry. But am I really settling down? It would seem that I stepped into a whirlwind that I have no control over. I can't clearly remember if I ever had the thought of making a home or not. It just seems to be creeping up on me. Will I be staying in the Texas Rangers? I always knew that one day I would have to give it up. But then again Bill Vents is as old as the hills, and he ain't give the Rangers up yet. The whole thing is so confusing that I don't seem to be able to control what's happening.

So without even thinking about it I unfolded my body from the chair and walked across the porch, onto the parade grounds and headed for downtown and the Zapata General Store. Moving towards whatever it is that's awaiting me.

It was still early, but Lola was out on the general store porch sweeping up, getting ready to open. She saw me from down the street and stopped what she was doing. Swung her hip to one side and put her hand on it like she had been waiting on me. As I drew closer, I could see the beginning of a smile cross her face and eyes.

"So, now you're coming visiting before we can even open the store. How do you know if I am prepared to be courted this early in the morning?" Lola asked.

Putting me off balance again, not knowing if I am doing the right thing or not. But I figured it had to be done, so I continued to the porch and grabbed Lola by the shoulders and planted a kiss right on her lips, long and hard.

"My, my Captain Creek! You are indeed a bold man."

"I now own a ranch just five hours or so out of town," I told her all a matter of fact like. "And I want you to ride out there with me right now. Don't go confusing me or playing with me, Lola."

"You're serious!" she exclaimed.

"As serious as a heart attack," I replied.

We arrived in the afternoon in the heat of the day. But there was a solid breeze blowing across the ridge dampening the force of the sun enough to make it bearable. When we rode to the top of the summit, we pulled our horses up and just sat there. I was taking the sight of the ranch in for the first time really. When I rode over here with Slim and Fred, I was still in shock, so it didn't look the same as it does now. It looked like some place I might just want to live.

"So what do you think, Lola?"

"I think you need to put a new roof on the barn. And paint the house. Did you buy this ranch to impress me so I'll marry you?" she asked me straight out, as bold as she could be.

I swear I have never met such a forward woman in my life. No matter what I say or do she makes me feel silly. Now she has made it worse by coming straight out and talking about getting hitched.

"I'll race you down!" Lola cried out as she put the spurs to her horse.

I didn't even try to outrun her. I was just enjoying seeing her ride with the view of the ranch in the background. We arrived at the front door of the ranch house in short order. Lola pulled up hard, sliding to a stop and slipped off her mount and in an instant, she was standing on the porch with her hands on her hips again. Laughing that deep laugh she has. You could almost feel it, making it impossible not to smile.

I stepped down off of Horse and walked up to the plank porch, and Lola came over and grabbed me by the hand and pulled me along to the kitchen. Then she dragged me over to the table and passed her arm across the top pushing the few items to the floor. Turning she pulled me to her, and she finally gave herself to me. Without a joke or hack one.

We stayed there in the house that night. Our blankets lay on the hardwood floor, but neither one of us paid much mind. Just happy to be alone without another thought in our minds. Maybe this ain't such a bad idea after all.

CHAPTER 5:

PEDRO MENDEZ

"¿Que?   Are you telling me what to do?" shouted Pedro Mendez at the sheriff of the Mexican town across the Rio Grande from El Paso.

Paso del Norte was an essential point of trade for Mexico.   Old Señor Mendez, as he obliged his employees to call him had amassed a vast amount of land over the years. And little by little he had populated it with Texan cattle. He even owned land north of the border and was a backer for the local Cattlemen's Association. Paying off whoever was necessary for him be allowed to continue to rebrand rustled cattle and horses from north of the border.

Pedro would send his thieves north to steal the cattle. Then they would take the livestock to Mexico. Place new brands over the old ones and register these modified brands. Then he had the cattle herded back to Texas to be sold at auction. As clean of an operation as a man could wish for. He was selling the same animals back to the men he stole them from. And all the time maintaining his image as a man of honor and a respected member of the Texas Cattlemen's Association. Claiming that he resided both in Mexico and Texas.

The fact was that old Mendez abhorred Texans one and all. He put on a show so he could continue to claim restitution against a people that had in fact stolen land from Mexico. The opinion south of the border was that the boundaries of the countries should have been farther north and not the Rio Grande. So old

Pedro continued to conduct guerrilla warfare with the Texans. But doing so in such a way that there were no repercussions against Señor Mendez himself. And in the process, he became richer and more prosperous.

But now he had heard that his activities had drawn the attention of the Texas Rangers. As he had his spy's in El Paso, Texas, he knew nearly every move that they made. He was aware of the contents of their telegrams and sometimes their mail. He even had spies in the banks and saloons. Even in Rosas Cantina which was secretly owned by Pedro Mendez himself. So he was keeping an eye on that shifty sumbitch, Captain Creek.

There was a time when he had all the law in El Paso in his pocket. That included Marshal Dallas Stoudenmire. But the presence of the Texas Rangers in the city had changed that. And it would appear that no one had ever been able to corrupt Ranger Creek. The Texan lawman had the tendency to shoot or hang any and all outlaws he encountered, so there was little time for negotiation.

The Mexican sheriff was just about to soil himself. He was more afraid of Mendez than any Texas Rangers but what Pedro was asking him to do was more than the man dared to attempt. Señor Mendez wanted him to take a substantial sum of money to the Texas Ranger Sergeants to see if he could corrupt them. Enabling Mendez to acquire information on the secret missions that Captain Creek organized against the horse and cattle rustling on the border.

Mendez had spent a substantial amount of money greasing the gears in Austin and had managed to install a corrupt Texas Ranger in the head office. Now he was maneuvering politicians in order to place his informant and inside man in the El Paso Texas Ranger Post. But if he could get someone like Sergeant Smith to turn and work for him, he would have total control over the border immediately. And if not, he would have to wait until his plant was provided and had time to gain the confidence of Captain Ridge Creek.

"No, Sir, Señor Méndez," the Mexican lawman replied quickly. "I just think that if I go directly to the two Ranger Sergeants and they refuse to take my bribe, they will figure out what is going on and maybe kill me. They may well be able to guess who it was that put me up to it too. That could be dangerous for us both. They say the two Rangers Smith and Vents have been with Captain Creek for decades. Especially the old man. It is hard to believe that a man would turn against his own after so many years."

"Money buys everybody!" Mendez refuted. "It may cost more for some than others, but every man has his price. You do as I say or you won't be working as town Sheriff next week. I kid you not."

"Yes Sir," the lawman replied.

But Jose Suarez had no intention of walking into a notorious Texas Ranger post and propose they take a bribe as his narcissist of a boss insisted. He would end up dead or at the very least hung right there in the post. So the Sheriff of Paso del Norte, Mexico took the only recourse he could. He packed his saddlebags and mounted up and rode off south towards safety and his family's homes well beyond the border. Here he was bound to end up dead at the hands of Pedro Mendez or the Texas Rangers, so the only hope for him was an escape.

Pedro Mendez had a long reach, but the town Jose was heading for would leave him lost in the Mexican masses. El Ciudad de Mexico. No one would be able to find him in such a massive population. It is easier to hide out amongst numbers than it is to hide out in some obscure village where everybody is going to notice a stranger. At some point or another Señor Mendez would find him. But in the big city, he could use a different name and probably avoid being murdered by the vicious old man.

After threatening the local sheriff, Pedro mounted his black stallion with a fancy Mexican saddle on it. It was covered in silver studs, and all the leather was decorated with intricate designs. A saddle that made people notice. As he turned his horse, he dug his fancy silver spurs into its flanks and led his men out of town on the south trail.

"I want you to send out three bunches of rustlers tonight," Pedro said to his right-hand man.

"Sí Señor," Marcos Sagrado replied. "I will see to it personally. Do you want me to go along, boss?"

"No, it is too dangerous. There will be Texas Rangers searching for our men on the border. If they catch one of our rustler parties, we will still have the profits of two. So it won't cost me a thing other than a few cowboys. Something that there is little shortage of here in Mexico. Just make sure that they don't know they are working for me. Now we must be more careful than ever. At least until I can have this Ranger Creek killed or out of the way. I'll have to work out a plan. I'm not going to allow anyone to stand in my way. That land should not belong to the Texans anyway. I feel if I continue to disrupt the border area maybe we can push the Texans back even more and I will have the land north of the border as well as on the southern side. I don't plan to allow a bunch of Texan heathens stand in the way of progress. We have been here for hundreds of years so what right do the Americans have to take our land?

CHAPTER 6:

HOG TIED

I walked into the chow hall during lunch knowing that I would find all of the men here at noon. I made my hand into a fist and banged on the open door to get their attention.

"Listen up gentlemen," I said. "We don't get paid to sit around in the Ranger post or to police

El Paso so first thing tomorrow morning we'll be riding out. That means everybody. Tonight clean and check all your weapons. There is a considerable amount of rustling going on between Texas and Mexico, and we need to see what we can do about it. And our old enemy Mister Lopez is said to be in the area. So keep your eyes peeled or you could get your life snatched away from you as quick as you can spit. I'll see you boys in the morning."

When I got back to my quarters I laid out my two Colt Walker pistols, my .44 caliber Paterson revolvers, the two Peacemakers and my .31 derringer and went about cleaning them, making sure everything was in order. I've been slacking off of late in regards to my job. In the past, I have always spent nearly all my time on one mission or another. But for the last weeks, I have spent more time with Miss Lola Zapata than working. Sometimes staying out at the ranch for a couple of days at a time.

Bill Vents had taken to staying at the ranch too. The Sergeant said he was just about done Rangering. He hired on as a Texas Ranger in 1823 when they were unofficially formed by Stephan F. Austin and headed by Captain Morris.

Then officially in 1835 when Daniel Parker created a unique body of Rangers to protect the Texan border with Mexico. Right up to today. He has been taking care of the Ranger pups for the last twenty years.

He always told me that when he got too old to set a bad example, he took to giving out good advice. If it weren't for Sergeant Vents, most of us wouldn't have lived as long as we have. Even the ones that have now passed had a little bit more time here on Earth with Bill watching over them. He's as pugnacious and cantankerous as a man can be, but he has always been as fine a person as I have ever had the pleasure to meet. And an exemplary comrade in a battle. Second only to Weston Smith.

Sergeant Smith has been my best friend for more than twenty years now. Weston is a bit older than me and was already a Corporal of the Texas Rangers when I signed on over two decades ago. I lied and said I was seventeen and as I had my own horse and was well armed they hired me without question. I reckon for me it was the best decision I've ever made. Even with the red rage that comes over me at times of violence. That too is a sort of blessing. It's why I have survived up to now. I may be scared up some and a few years older, but everything works as well as when I was twenty. And my skills with my guns are even better.

The next morning every man on the post was standing beside his horse waiting for me to mount up and twirl my two fingers. That was enough to put the patrol into motion and out we went riding along the border.

"We're going to ride right by the ranch, Captain," Bill Vents said when we pulled out in front of the column. "Don't hurt to ride by. I like looking at it from up on Windy Ridge."

"You better get your mind back on the job and stop thinking about what might be. If we ain't careful, we not might be. Let's ride wide of ranch and tend to our business."

So we avoided our new home away from home for the moment. It's best for me to stick to business so my mind doesn't start to drift back to thoughts of Lola which out here could cost a man his life. Bill, Weston and I headed the formation with a single file of Rangers following. Rowdy Bates at the head of the boys with Toby

Bees, Humphrey, and Clinton and all the rest of the men trailing behind.

"I ain't seen Tuc or Potak so far, Ridge," Weston commented.

"Just because you don't see them don't mean that they ain't out there watching out for us," Sergeant Vents stated. "I reckon if Toby Bees is in our patrol and the outlaw Lopez is about those two Tonkawa are somewhere out there too. They have been protecting Toby ever since he signed on."

"Lopez could be long gone by now," Weston pondered. "I ain't never seen him stick around when he is in Texas or just over the border for long. He has every lawman in both countries looking for him."

"Problem is that all the law south of the border is so scared of the man that they don't speak a word about him," I replied. "I have heard of Lopez taking revenge on entire families for going to the law to rat him out. Some say he even kills their friends. Sends a strong message that. Especially to the poor Mexican peasant folks that are just trying to get by in life. Ain't no point of signing a man's death warrant by flapping their jaw about an outlaw as nefarious as Lopez."

"I figure that we will ride parallel to the river for half the day then we can hold up at the old Ranger camp on that hill so we have a good view of the Rio Grande," I continued. "We can sleep in shifts and make like we are settling down for the night. Then we can saddle up and move on out around midnight. There is a Comanche Moon tonight so we can make our way along the trail that heads east and not be seen. If we run into any rustlers, we can grab the lot and drive them back towards El Paso."

"What if we run into Lopez?" Weston asked as he had a look around him just to be on the safe side. "Hell, he could be waiting out there right now what with you sending that message with the Indian gossip. Telling him, you're coming to kill him and all. I doubt he takes kindly to the comment."

"I don't care if he takes kindly to it or not," I retorted. "I intended to rile the man up a bit to see if he makes a mistake."

"He usually just gets meaner when he is riled up," Weston implored.

"And that is when he's most careless," I added. "We nearly got him that one time when we ran him and his men south from Texas. The only reason he escaped is he sacrificed pretty much all his men up around that canyon in the process. But even that was by design and not by accident. Never forget how intelligent that man is or how willing he is to sacrifice his own men to save his hide."

"It was your Winchester that almost got him that day," Bill Vents said. "Just like on Kiowa Hill the enemy didn't expect it. It cost Lopez his best two men to boot and if not for the luck of the devil the bushwhacking sumbitch wouldn't have got away."

"But he did," I replied. "Like he has been doing for the last twenty years. He must be about forty some odd years old now. Maybe he ain't as sharp as he was last we met."

"You've aged the same, Captain and I ain't seen you get nothing but meaner in battle," Weston acknowledged.

"If we do run into Lopez you best not be running off and doing anything crazy now, Ridge. You got Lola to think of now. And our ranch," Bill responded. "The last few scraps we've had you have gone off with that red rage you get into, but it takes you much longer to come back to normal. If you're not careful, one day you might start to see red and not stop. Then what are we going to do?"

"You worry too damned much, old man," Sergeant Smith snickered. "I reckon you're right, thinking about being put out to pasture and all."

"Why I could outfight you any day of the week you young whippersnapper," Vents snorted. "Even at my age, so you best mind your manners."

We rode on through the twilight finally stopping at a point on top of a hill where a rustlers' trail passed. There were many such trails that the rustlers use to move back and forth unperceived with small herds of cattle. But this was one of the most used due the easier crossing of the river that it provided.

I pulled out my telescope and extended it to its full length. Old Sergeant Henry Hunt's spyglass that I kept after he ran off into a tornado like some kind of man possessed. As I watched, I saw a small herd of some forty cattle start to move down a hill from the Texan side of the border. The men wore Mexican sombreros. Rustlers, stealing cattle from Texans to sell to Pedro Mendez in Mexico.

I turned and looked back at the men all now crouched down waiting for their orders.

"Bill, you take Rangers Billy Joe James and Travis Picket and swing around them and get on the east side to keep them from running that way. Weston, you take Rowdy, Humphrey, and Ace and move down the hill here on the west side of the rustlers. Both of you men wait down near the river. The cattle are moving slowly so you should have time to get there before them and still go undetected. When you are both in place, Weston you shoot off your two revolvers, and we will come at them hard from behind. We'll have them in a crossfire if they run. And if they stand and fight I'll deal with them with Clinton and Toby.

"We'll stay with you Captain Creek," Tuc said making Weston nearly jump out of his skin.

"You two have got to stop sneaking up on us like that!" Weston implored. "I swear that I'll shoot you one of these days."

"We didn't sneak up on you," Potak refuted. "It's no fault of ours that you weren't paying attention."

"Let's go, men," I ordered as I mounted Horse and pulled his reins to the right and started to ride over to the path the rustlers were taking to drive the cattle down the hill and across the Rio Grande. "Toby, Humphrey, and Clinton follow me slow and quiet now. We don't want them to see or hear us although the sound of the cattle will cover most of our noise. Especially if we're careful."

So down the hill we rode with me taking the lead, Toby behind me and in front of Humphrey and his scatter-gun. Then following up the rear was Clinton Westwood. As usual daydreaming about something. That or asleep in the saddle and this ain't the time to act in such a manner. But Clinton was one of those fellers that were convinced that nothing but good luck and fortune was headed his way. It was just a matter of when. So he spent his time procrastinating on most jobs he is ordered to do. And sits down and goes to sleep every chance he gets. Even when he is mounted on top of his horse.

"Make sure that Clinton is awake back there," I said to Toby as I turned in the saddle.

But Clinton Westwood was nowhere to be seen and with limited visibility at night and us in the middle of starting an outlaw roundup, I couldn't take the time to find out where he had dozed off too.

"He just up and vanished, boss," Toby whispered.

"We'll tend to it in due time, son," I replied as I kept my eyes peeled on the rustlers. "One thing at a time. Our Rangers down by the river are counting on us to bring up the rear, so there is no going back now. Westwood will have to wait till we have caught the rustlers."

We moved down the hill at a quicker pace expecting the pistol shots from Weston at any minute. Then suddenly two shots rang out in the night so we spread out best we could on the trail and headed holus-bolus towards the

Mexican cattle rustlers. As soon as they saw us four racing after them with our Winchesters pointing their way they started to shoot off their pistols to stampede the small herd of rustled cattle towards the river. Yelling and shouting to spook the animals.

But as they neared the river rifle fire began to come from their right and left flanks as Weston's and Bill's positions got them in a crossfire. Two of the rustlers went down right off. Shot in the chest and back quicker than you could blink. Both shots by Rowdy Bates which made the remaining rustlers have a change of heart, and they dropped their weapons and put their hands in the air. There had been six men in all, with two now dead.

"Grab the Mexican's guns and tie their hands behind their backs with pigging string and keep them mounted," I ordered. "Let's push this herd north along with the rustlers. We can deal with them in El Paso. Weston, you and Bill, take the cattle as far as Windy Ridge Ranch. You can put them in the coral for now. I'm going looking for Clinton Westwood. Rowdy, Toby and Humphrey come with me. The rest of you all go along with the herd. And keep sharp. Lopez might be out there somewhere."

Rowdy Bates, Toby Bees and I had our pistols in hand as the two young Rangers, Humphrey, and I rode back up the way we came. Moving slowly with care in the case there are some Comanche or outlaws about. We got to where we noticed Clinton was gone, but there was not a sign one of where he got off to.

"Let's start riding in circles men. Each time you complete a circle move out some more until we can pick up the tracks. Be careful now as I figure we got hostiles out here with us."

As soon as I said hostiles Ranger Willow pulled back the two hammers of his scatter-gun making that metallic click. The double barrel lay in the crook of his stump of an arm.

We rode around in circles for nearly twenty minutes before we found Clinton's horse. He had been stabbed in the neck so he wouldn't make any noise when he died. With the stampeded cattle and gunshots, I doubt we would have heard if the horse had been shot.

"This ain't looking good for Clinton," Humphrey said. "Those are boot prints over there, so I doubt it's Comanche. It's probably the outlaw Lopez that done got him. Damn, now I feel for that young man even if he is generally a pain in the ass. The cockamamie damned fool."

"We ain't found him dead yet," I implored.

"How many men have you rescued from Lopez over the years, boss?" Humphrey Willow asked.

I looked at him with a hard stare and replied, "None."

———

Clinton Westwood was following Humphrey Willow, but he wasn't really paying much attention to where they were going. He figured that six Mexican cowboys were no match for ten Texas Rangers. Especially as we got the drop on them and Captain Creek is with us.

When the tomahawk came in quick towards Clinton's skull, he only saw the blur in his side vision, and then nothing but stars as he fell right off his horse and suddenly saw the ground come up to meet his head. Half unconscious he was still aware that he was being dragged by his boots, off the trail and his horse was following the man who had captured the young Texas Ranger.

The kidnapper didn't make a sound as he rushed through the night. His drooping mustache and long hair visible with the Comanche Moon. When he looked back at Clinton, the young man could see the whites of his black eyes in the dim light. That and the wicked grin on his face looking more like a jackal than any other critter that walks on two or four legs.

As soon as they were a short distance from where Lopez had hit the Texas Ranger, he pulled Clinton's horse close and plunged a huge bowie knife into his neck, cutting the juggler vein, and the animal dropped to the ground like a limp sack of potatoes. Clinton opened his mouth in protest, but another sound thump on the head with the stone tomahawk was more than the

Ranger could tolerate before he lost total consciousness.

"There are a lot of men walking around with tombstones in their eyes, Gringo," Lopez whispered. "Tonight is the night that I'll kill With Dead Eyes. And as many Rangers as I can murder along with him."

If possible, he planned to kill all those lawmen. Lopez hated the Texas Rangers, but this hate mostly stemmed from Captain Ridge Creek. Creek had killed his two best men and a couple of dozen of his outlaws over the years. Sure Lopez had killed several of the Captain's Rangers too. He hadn't counted, but it was more than a handful, although now he wanted the big prize. Lopez had been told that With Dead Eyes was out here looking for him. Well, here he was right here waiting.

He hog-tied the Ranger and lashed him to a stake to make sure he couldn't move. Then Lopez vanished into the night to capture his next Texas Ranger. The main group had ridden off north with the herd of stolen cattle that Lopez had sent the rustlers to take. He knew they would get caught, but he also figured that one of the Rangers would get reckless with such an easy task. And he was right. The last man in the formation was nearly asleep when he hit him in the head.

After a spell of moving through the night, Lopez could hear the horses circling near where he captured the Ranger. He found a spot to hide and waited for his chance.

What he didn't see was Tuc hiding in a shadow not too far from the villain. Pulling back his bowstring as he waited for his opportunity. Lopez was focused on Toby Bees and not worrying about someone else being out here hiding in the dark. Tuc was the true master of the night. Living most of his time in the shadows.

The Tonkawa Indian let the arrow fly but at that very instant Lopez lunged for Sergeant Bees as he sat astride his horse. The piece of wood and stone penetrated deep into the thigh of the Mexican outlaw. But with the reflexes of a cat, he pushed Toby aside and to the ground and jumped onto and straddled the Sergeant's horse and took off like a bat out of hell. Riding right through the mist of the Texas Rangers.

Potak was at Toby's side in seconds. Crouching over him to give him cover were Lopez able to get a shot off with his revolver. Tuc shot off another arrow into the night, but they heard no sound other than the escaping hooves of Toby's favorite horse, Dusty.

"Are you alright, Toby?" I asked the shaken Ranger.

"I'm fine, Captain. We best go see if we can find Clinton. I hope he ain't all cut up like the other Rangers that Lopez captured."

Tuc and Potak moved through the night tracking the signs that Lopez left before the attack on Sergeant Bees. Finally coming to the squirming body of Clinton Westwood. Hog-tied but trying like the dickens to get loose. Tuc crouched down and looked at the young Ranger and shook his head.

"You're too careless," Tuc said as he pulled the gag from the Ranger's mouth. "Normally you should be dead now."

I rode up just as Tuc spoke and said, "That is a fact Ranger Westwood. By all rights, you should be skint and killed by now. I told you that your sleeping on duty was going to get you buried. Death keeps no calendar."

"He just came up on me before I knew it," Clinton explained. "He was so fast I didn't have time to react. I saw his face up close too. It was like looking into the eyes of the Devil himself. I reckoned for sure that I was dead meat."

"You and me both!" Toby Bees exclaimed. "If it weren't for Tuc he would have got me too. That man has some cajones to come at us on his own and all. He could make an ordinary fight look like a prayer meeting."

"You keep in mind for the future that death never takes a wise man by surprise," I said to Clinton. "He is always ready to go. You're too lax, lazy and you're a far from wise, son."

"Let's get out of here," Humphrey Willow said. "It gives me the jitters being out here when I know Lopez is about."

CHAPTER: 7

LOLA ZAPATA

As the four of us arrived at the Windy Ridge Ranch, we could see that the corral was full of stock. All the cattle that had been rustled and the horses from the outlaws. Toby was riding double with Clinton as Lopez the outlaw done stole Dusty, his horse.

"I bought plenty of supplies, Captain," Ranger Willow said. "I'll have some fried eggs, hash-brown potatoes and biscuits made up in a jiffy, boss. The boys should have a pot of coffee already made up."

Riding down to the ranch house did make me feel different. Arriving at a place I own rather than my regular home which is a barracks quarters along with the rest of the Rangers. Like all of a sudden, a quiet settled life may be in the cards for me. Albeit along with Bill, Weston, and Humphrey, although with only Lola to help me we wouldn't' be able to build much of a ranch on our own. It takes ranch hands to tend to the stock and with my Captain's job I would be stretched far too thin to be able to tend to the task alone. And who could deny old Bill Vents a bit of peace and relaxation after all he has done for us Texas Rangers over the years.

As we rode up, I noted that a dozen chairs had now been procured from one place or another. Most likely part of them come from the Ranger post chow hall. Weston and Bill were sitting there drinking hot coffee.

"Well, I see that you found Clinton," Weston stated. "I was kind of hoping that Lopez would do away with him so we won't have to look after him so much."

"The ranch looks like it's a working business with stock in the corral and all," I said to Bill and Weston.

"I figure we can keep the rustler's horses and maybe a few heads of cattle for our troubles," Bill Vents added. "I don't mind hanging around and tending to the livestock."

"We ought to go down to Mexico at night and rustle a bunch of cattle from the men who stole them in the first place," Weston said. "We could stock the ranch in three or four trips. Few dozen horses and a few hundred head of cattle."

"Don't you two think you're being a bit too ambitious all of a sudden?" I asked as I stepped down off of my mount and tied the reins to the hitching rail.

"I'm tired of rubbing my back-sides on saddle leather," Bill retorted. "I need a good home and some rest."

"All right then," I replied. "Don't go getting all angry on us. I was just saying."

"This is the first time that I've ever had the opportunity to sit back and relax a bit, and I aim to make use of it," Bill snorted. "A man that's been Rangering as long as I have deserved something in life."

"Alright, Bill," I replied. "Whatever you say, Sergeant. Now let's see what we can put together in the way of grub. I'm so hungry could eat a bear."

Travis Picket came over and tended to our horses, and the four of us grabbed a chair and sat down to enjoy a hot cup of coffee along with a few of the boys.

"Did you kill him, Ridge?" Weston asked. "I figured it was Lopez as soon as we left with the rustlers."

"No, I didn't kill the sumbitch. He got away again. At least he didn't kill any of our boys this time, although it sure was a close call for Westwood. What did you do with those four outlaws?" I asked.

"We don't have no jail cell, so I chained them to the blacksmith's anvil we got here on the ranch. They ain't going nowhere fast." Weston replied.

"Billy Joe, when you're done with your coffee go on into town to the Marshal's office and ask Stoudenmire what he wants to do with the horse thieves," I ordered. "We can leave the decision up to him. I tired of deciding if a man is to live or die. I reckon that Lopez put those six men up to stealing the cattle just to lure me in close. He is as clever as a rat that scoundrel."

In short order, Humphrey made true to his word. We had hash browned frying pan potatoes, frying pan biscuits and fried eggs, sunny side up just the way I like them.

"I got some nice big apples baking in the oven, boss," Humphrey said. "I figured we'd work on that sweet tooth of yours a bit."

"Sounds fine indeed, Ranger Willow," I replied as I broke off a bit of biscuit and dipped it in the yellow of one of my eggs.

"What's the plan now Captain?" Weston asked.

"We go right back out and look for more rustlers," I replied. "I have a mind to ride just over the river and follow the south trail till we run into another bunch of horse and cattle thieves."

"Lookee over yonder, boss," Humphrey said pointing to the top of Windy Ridge. "Ain't that Miss Zapata heading our way in a buggy?"

"It looks like those plans you had to head right back out may not be in your own best interest, Ridge," Weston said with a snicker.

"Now that Lola has shown up I figure you're right about me," I said. "But that don't keep you boys from going out and continuing with the mission. We ain't done here by a long shot."

"Oh, come on now Captain," Weston complained. "We can go out any old time. It's as easy as spit finding rustlers south of the border."

"You boys head back out just before dark, so you make the river right after dusk," I ordered. "Cross into northern Mexico and see how you fare but make sure you don't go over a mile or two south without me with you. With any luck, you will be back with some more cattle and horses. Maybe even an outlaw or three."

"Can I pick my own men?" Sergeant Smith asked.

"No need to make a pick as everybody is going back out with you," I replied. "Except for me as I am sure that Lola won't be allowing me to leave just right now. Not me traipsing off as soon as she shows up here to visit."

I unwound my tall frame from the chair after I hastily finished my breakfast, so I was done before Lola's buggy got to the ranch house.

"What are you doing riding all the way from El Paso to the ranch all on your own, Sweetie Pie?" I asked. "It ain't safe for such a fine woman as yourself to be out on the trail all on your lonesome."

Lola pulled up in front of the hitching post and stood in the buggy to show me she was sporting a light caliber revolver in a fine leather holster at the front of her dress.

"So now you have taken to wearing a pistol?" I asked.

"Well, it certainly isn't my first time. It's just that up to now you haven't seen me sporting a revolver. I know how to use it too," she said defiantly.

"I don't like you riding out here all on your own," I replied dead serious. "There's an evil outlaw about at the moment, and if he catches you, it will be horrible. The same man got ahold of Clinton Westwood on our last patrol, and it nearly cost him his life. That man has killed a handful of my Rangers in the past."

"You worry too much," Lola retorted. "Most folks worry all their lives over something that probably will never happen."

"Arguing with you is like picking a bone with a tree stump. You don't listen to a word I say."

"I certainly do listen but only when you have something interesting to talk about," she said as she put her hands on her hips and gave that deep laugh of hers, defiant as usual.

"I'd swear you're the most contrary woman that I have ever met!"

"Be that as it may I bet that I am also the most beautiful Mexican woman that you have ever met. Am I not correct, Captain Ridge Creek?"

"That you are darling," I replied as I walked over to take Lola's hand and help her down off of the buggy.

"I was thinking of taking you for a picnic tomorrow. If we follow the creek upstream towards the lake, about halfway there is a small pond where the water falls over some rocks. It's crystal clear, and it has a thatch of trees around the pond. I saw it on a ride up to Slim Pickens ranch, the Double HH. I'll have Humphrey make up a mess of food for us before he goes out on patrol tonight. I figure we could spend the whole day."

"Why, that is awfully sweet of you, Honey. I can't think of another thing that I would rather do."

"Have a seat then sugar plum, and I tell Humphrey to make up tomorrow's picnic, and I'll bring you a nice hot cup of coffee."

That night the Rangers all lit out and left Lola and me alone. The ranch house had a large sitting room with an attached kitchen and fireplace. In addition, it had two more rooms. One was made up for Lola and me, and the other had been converted into a bunkhouse for Weston, Humphrey and of course Bill Vents. There were a few extra bunk-beds for any of the boys that might show up on a day off. If there weren't enough room, the boys would throw out their bedrolls on the sitting room floor and bunk there. It was better than sleeping under the stars as it gets chilly out here at night near the mountains. And the sitting room had a big fireplace. One of Sergeant Vent's favorite spots to spin his yarns.

Lola and I slept in late the next day, enjoying the special occasion for just the two of us to be here at the ranch all alone. Usually, there was a passel of Rangers around whenever we are together. That or her family when I visited her in the general store. But today we didn't make it out of bed until after half past nine. I personally can't ever remember getting up so late. And it was not something that I planned to inform my men of. But with Lola it was special. Just being lazy for a change. A feeling that I have rarely had in my lifetime.

Around noon we saddled up the horses as the trail along the creek-bed is not suitable for a buggy. But it's a clear trail that winds along with the flow of the stream. In a couple of hours, we were at the spot I had picked for today's outing. We laid out a large blanket under the biggest tree right on the water's edge. Lola was already fussing about over the food that Humphrey had prepared for us and put in a basket that I had slung over the saddle horn on Horse's saddle to bring along.

Fried chicken, boiled corn on the cob, baked potatoes, and a whole peach pie. My, did we ever have a feast. Just talking idle chit-chat as we ate and passed the afternoon. Lola never stopped talking about one thing or another, but that was fine by me. That way I didn't say anything stupid like I usually do. But today I was feeling my oats and suddenly jumped to my feet and started pulling off my boots.

"What are you doing, Ridge?" Lola asked with a snicker.

"I'm going to have me a swim, girl. The last one in has to clear up the mess from the picnic."

So I skinned out of my clothing and dove straight into the small pond. It was so shallow that when I came up I could sit down and my head was still out of the water.

"Come on, girl. Get your butt in here with me."

After a moment of thought Lola did as I said and she too skinned out of her clothes and joined me in the fresh, clear water. We were still close enough to the bank to enjoy the shade of the tree. A slight breeze rustled the leaves making a pleasant calming sound. The only other sound was that of the splashing water that Lola made as she swam to the other side.

"What are you swimming for?" I asked. "You can walk all the way across the pond without getting your hair wet."

"You can, but I'm only five-feet-six so you've got more than a half a foot on me, Honey" Lola replied.

We spent the entire afternoon there, playing with each other, sparking and courting the whole day long. At times throughout the day, thoughts of my life as a Texas Ranger would come to me, and I would wonder how long could such peacefulness last. I have spent over two decades fighting to hold the peace with both the outlaws and the local Indian Tribes. Hardly ever a dull moment and rarely an extra week to take off. Making me wonder if the violence is done or will it be something that I will never be able to escape? As long as men like Lopez are around it seems hard to believe.

CHAPTER 8:

COMANCHE VILLAGE

"Stop all that commotion outside the door!" Bertha Bogardus shouted out to the impatient Comanche Braves that were waiting outside her tee-pee lodge.

The big red-haired Scottish woman seemed to have taken charge of the camp. She had her own lodge in the village and as many bearskin blankets to lay on as she wanted. Her Indian suitors had showered gifts on her hoping that she would select one or another of the Warrior Braves that had taken a shining to the bodacious Scotswoman. But she ran through men like shit through a goose. Bedding each one and then turning him away for another Indian Brave.

The Comanche all had designs on making Bertha one of their wives. But one after another was sent off packing once Bertha was done with them. She seemed earnest enough when it came to getting hitched, but she just kept saying that none of the men in the camp had tickled her fancy. So she kept up with the selection process much to the disgruntled annoyance of the Braves, but to the absolute delight of Bertha herself.

Bertha Bogardus was a woman who had been starved for affection her entire life in Glasgow, Scotland. Her father dismissed the woman, saying that she was mentally challenged and locked her up in the castle. Denying her the same rights that he allowed Seth her brother. He was not any more intelligent than her although not quite so promiscuous when it came to sexual favors. Bertha's appetite for carnal needs seemed to be endless.

Some of the old man Bogardus intellect did live inside Bertha. In just a short time she had already learned a considerable number of Comanche words and could defend herself with her limited vocabulary and sign language. The men seemed to have no problem understanding the Scotswoman. They appeared to all be so fascinated with her red hair and large breasts that they were all competing for the European prize.

On the other side of the village, five Comanche Braves sat smoking a pipe and talking. They actually seemed to be arguing to some degree over the Bogardus woman.

"Ever since we made contact with that old Scottish man nothing but bad has befallen the village," Mukwooru said. "The behavior of that woman is unacceptable."

"You try to tell that to the Warriors," Topsannah replied.

"I brought the white woman to the camp," Panayoko said. "She should be mine and not belong to some other Brave."

"You should have killed her with the others," Huupi-Panati added.

"If you kill her now you may well be the one that loses his scalp," Lucky Ha-Ha said with a chortle.

"Between that red-haired white woman and the two wagons full of liquor our camp has become unruly," Mukwooru snorted. "No one wants to follow orders. None of the Braves want to leave the camp and go out and hunt or make raids. We should have let the wagon-train pass and left them alone."

"It was that Tonkawa that told us we could take whatever we wanted from the wagon-train," Huupi-Panati said. "We should have known better than to trust a Tonkawa. He may be taking revenge for what we did to his people, driving them all away to northern Kansas."

As the men sat around a fire and smoked their pipe and spoke, Bertha Bogardus spotted Panayoko, the man who had brought her here to the Comanche village and moved in his direction at a furious pace. Her face was almost as red as her hair. The white woman stormed up to the five men and stomped the ground to get their attention. Standing before the heads of the tribe with her hands made into fists and perched on her hips.

"You are responsible, Panayoko," she declared. "You brought me here against my own free will, and I demand that you release me right now."

"I brought you here to be my wife, and you came willingly," the Comanche retorted. "If you want to go, then go. Take one of the horses we stole and leave. The big black stallions of your fathers have not been eaten yet so take them. The Braves don't like those horses. They are not adequate animals for Comanche Territory."

"Go ahead and leave," Mukwooru ordered. "We don't want you here. Huupi-Panati, go over and burn the wagons with the liquor in them. Burn everything. I want all sign of the Scottish man removed from our village before the sun sets."

"Come on, Bertha," Panayoko said. "I will go with you halfway to make sure you arrive safely. Let's go get your horses."

The Comanche Warrior and the redheaded white woman made their way along a winding path that led through the Indian camp. All the women looked at Bertha Bogardus like they wanted to kill her. But they would settle with her leaving. So nobody interfered with the woman's departure. Everybody but a half dozen Comanche men that had not had the opportunity to prove themselves as good husbands.

"What about us?" one of six Warrior Braves asked. "We have not had our turn yet."

"Go on and get out of here," Panayoko said to the inebriated Comanche. "This business with the white woman and the liquor is over."

In short order, the Comanche was mounted on his spotted Indian pony, and Bertha sat astride a beautiful black Arabian stallion with an identical horse following. They rode out of the camp at a gallop. Bertha knew very well where she was headed next in her new life. El Paso will be her new destination.

They rode most of the way to Six-Gun-City, using Comanche raiding trails to avoid being spotted by the Texas Rangers or armed ranchers. When they were as close as Panayoko dared go, he pulled the horses up.

"Are you sure that you don't want to be my wife, Bertha?" the Comanche Warrior asked the red-haired woman. "I still want to marry you."

"I have no intention of marrying you or any man at the moment. I intend to spend some time in El Paso. I can tend to my father's business and sell off the ranch in New Mexico, me being the next heir in line for the inheritance. I believe that it should be worth a small fortune so it will provide me with money for the time being. When I run out, I may well return to Scotland where I will take over all my father's possessions. Making me vastly rich. Now I can finally do whatever I want to."

"Go on then!" he snapped. "If you return to our camp you will surely be killed by Mukwooru, so you have been warned."

With that, the Comanche Warrior Brave turned his horse and rode off heading back south and towards the Indian village. He never looked back once to check on Bertha. Nor did she pay any attention to the man's departure. She was now happy as a lark and was singing an old Scottish folk song as she made her way to the six-gun capital of the West.

When she rode into town, she headed to the livery stables and had her two Arabian stallions tended to. The old man at the stables eyed the strange red-haired woman with the Indian buckskins.

"Where can I find a place to bathe, a general store to purchase some new clothing and the best dancehall in town?" she asked.

"The Zapata General Store and Haberdashery is just down the street, Ma-am," Mister McContrary the liveryman replied. "And the biggest saloons in town are the Black Water and Rosa's Cantina. And there's a bathhouse right next door."

"Thank you very much, Mister," Bertha added and headed off to locate the general store.

She intended to acquire some new fancy clothing more suitable for her intended city life here in El Paso. She didn't have any money at the moment, but she was sure that she would be given credit when the owners consider with whom they are dealing. Her family was known for its vast fortunes across the globe, and now it was all hers.

As she walked down the street full of purpose she saw the general store and headed that way. Head down, fists clenched and jaw set. A determined woman who would not accept anything short of her desires. She stepped up onto the porch just when a beautiful Mexican woman walked through the door.

"Good morning, Miss," Lola Zapata said greeting the woman despite her strange manner of dress. "What can I do for you this fine morning?"

The red-haired Scottish woman stuck out her hand and said, "My name is Bertha Bogardus, the daughter of the late Lord Bogardus. I am in need of a completely new wardrobe if you would be so kind as to assist me. I am afraid that at this precise moment I don't have any cash on hand, but I assure that you will be taken care of directly. You do know with whom you are speaking, do you not dear?"

"Actually I am quite aware of who you are Miss Bogardus," Lola replied with a sly smile. "My gentleman friend is Captain Creek of the Texas Rangers. He was sent to rescue you father in the Comanche village. I am sorry that was something that was not possible. I commiserate with you on your loss, Ma-am."

"No sense crying over spilled milk, dear," Bertha replied as happy as a dog with a new bone. "I would like to look at dresses. The fancier, the better. Low cut in the bosom would be my preference."

Lola looked at the woman with a knowing smile and replied, "I do believe that I know just what you are looking for."

CHAPTER 9:

RUSTLING CATTLE

The Texas Ranger patrol didn't ride out of the Windy Ridge Ranch until about midnight. Captain Creek was still up to see the men off, although Sergeants Weston Smith and Bill Vents were able-bodied lawmen and could take care of whatever situation they may encounter. At the moment they were heading out to look for

Mexicans that were rustling cattle just north of the border and driving them back south to sell to Pedro Mendez. The most prominent rancher in the Paso del Norte, Mexico area. The orneriest one as well.

As they headed south each of the nine Texas Rangers keep their eyes peeled. They were on the lookout for cattle rustlers, but they also knew that Lopez had been in the vicinity recently. Especially Clinton Westwood.

"I have a bad feeling about this mission," he said to Toby Bees and Rowdy Bates.

"You're just worried because that rascal Lopez caught you," Toby replied. "You're as lucky a man as I have ever met. I have seen Lopez catch more than one Ranger and torture them to death. He is one mean hombre that Mexican feller."

"Luck is something that a man has to understand to avoid the bad luck," Rowdy explained. "I have managed to steer clear of bad luck most of the time up till now. Then again there is blind luck which is what saved your bacon, Clinton. Luck ain't to be despised."

"I'd feel better if the Captain were here with us," Clinton added. "Us going down across the border and all. Just about anything could happen to us on this mission. We could one, and all perish as quickly as you can spit."

"You ain't growing a yellow streak are you, Westwood?" Rowdy Bates asked. "You best focus on doing your job and let the Sergeants worry about the mission. That's what they are here for."

"Life is short and full of blisters," Toby added.

The men rode on crossing the Rio Grande and entered into Mexico under the light of the half moon. Every single Ranger's eyes and ears were focused on any out of place movements or sounds. After about an hour into Mexico Weston and Bill heard a familiar whistle.

"That will be Potak making his bird calls," Bill Vents said. "Hopefully they will have some news for us on where some rustlers might be."

Like two phantoms the Tonkawa, Tuc, and Potak came into sight. At first, they appeared hazy in the moonlight. Then, as they came closer, the moonlight reflected on Tuc's gruesome grin. Making the two look like ghoulish apparitions floating across the landscape.

"Hell, now I'm just plain scared," Clinton said.

"Why it is just Tuc and Potak," Toby replied. "I always feel safer when they're around. I was wondering when they would turn up. It is a rare occasion that I go out on a mission, and they don't show up beside the trail or come out of some shadows.

"Soon you're going to be clucking like an old hen," Rowdy said to Clinton. "Scared of your own shadow. Texas Rangers are supposed to be fearless. I have been riding with Captain Creek for quite a spell now and I ain't never seen him whine or falter. The Sergeants neither."

"Don't keep hacking on Clinton like that," Toby retorted in a hushed voice. "He just got captured by Lopez, the outlaw. If it had happened to you, I bet you would be a bit shy of danger too."

"That is exactly my point, Toby," Sergeant Bates said. "Something like that would never happen to me as I don't ride around asleep on my horse all the time. Especially when nefarious characters like Lopez are around."

"The boss making you Captain of the Laredo Ranger post is going to your head," Toby said with a snicker. "Next you will be running for town mayor. Wouldn't that be something? You sure do have an imagination, Mister Bates. I couldn't count the times I caught you sleeping while riding patrol back when we signed up."

"Well, now things are different. I have new responsibilities. A man given such a chance in life has to rise to the occasion. And it has been a long time since you have seen me lazy, Mister Bees."

Up in the front of the column, Tuc and Potak rode up beside Sergeants Smith and Vents. Both men comfortable with the two Tonkawa coming out of the shadows unannounced. It was rare these days that these two scouts don't show up before the men get to trouble.

"Got anything to tell up boys?" Bill Vents asked the two Indians. "Seen any horse or cattle thieves out there tonight."

"Stop and wait here," Tuc said in a whisper. "It won't be long, now."

Nor did it surprise the Sergeants when Tuc told them to sit and wait. Although at times Tuc was less than honest and he did have the tendency of collecting bits and pieces of his enemies. But the man was a devil of a fighter, and if he said to stop and wait, there would be a good reason to do so.

"Everybody dismount," Sergeant Smith said in a quiet voice. "Stand at the ready, gentlemen. We are about to have company."

Twenty minutes time hadn't passed when they all heard the noise of a slow-moving herd of cattle. The rustlers, now on Mexican land never expected the Texas Rangers to be waiting in the dark as they leisurely moved the animals towards the agreed to destination. To turn the cows and horses over to Pedro Mendez's men.

"Rowdy, break off five men and ride to the other side of the trail," Weston ordered. "Let's take them alive if they are willing. Only shoot if you have to, so we don't let everybody in Mexico know we're here."

"Come on boys," Rowdy said to the five Rangers to his left.

The patrol was now split up as the small herd of about a sixty head passed between the men. Five Mexican cowboys were riding the cattle. Two on both sides and one to the rear.

The last rider was pushing the herd making sure that no strays wander off along the trail. He didn't even see the Indian who shot the arrow. The handcrafted projectile sailed through the air at a remarkable speed but in complete silence. The only indication that the arrow was fired being the grunt of the cowboy when it pierced his heart. It passed clear through his chest, the arrowhead sticking out of the back of his shirt. The rustler wobbled for a moment before he fell from his horse. Tuc immediately ran over to the outlaw and removed his ears with a long fine knife. Stuffing them into a leather pouch he had tied to his gun belt.

"You know what the Captain said about cutting your enemies up, Tuc," Potak complained. "You're always looking to get us into trouble."

"Captain Creek ain't here is he? Sergeant Smith never gives us orders like With Dead Eyes does. You're always worrying about things you imagine might happen. Pay attention to what you're doing. Get the man's guns."

On each flank, the Rangers rushed at the rustlers from the shadows. All four men were so surprised that they didn't even go for their guns. When they saw the beige hats, they stuck their hands up in the air. Surrendering simply due to the confusion of the surprise. None of the outlaws ever imagining Texan lawmen coming into Mexico to catch a few horse rustlers.

"Rowdy, turn that herd around and head them back towards the border," Weston ordered. "Toby, see that these four men get their hands tied. I don't want any of them running off. Now stay quiet men. We'll be back in Texas lickety-split."

As Sergeants Smith and Vents rode to the front of the herd of cattle, they came upon Tuc and Potak. They were just walking away from the body of the Mexican rustler.

"What'd you kill that man for, Tuc?" Weston asked.

"You said not to shoot our guns," the scout replied. "I didn't use my guns."

"Well, what's done is done. Let's head on home and get these cattle back to Windy Ridge."

When they got to the Windy Ridge Ranch, there wasn't enough space in the corral to fit all the stock. So the Captain ordered some of the Rangers to get to work on making a larger coral and the rest of the boys to ride the herd until they had someplace to put them.

"I figure that if we keep fifty head of each group of rustled cattle we are up a hundred head," Weston said all a matter of fact like. "With the brands changed they ain't going to ever figure out who they belong to anyway. Ain't no branding logs that is going to include doctored brands from south of the border."

"That is a fact," Bill Vents agreed. "And I am just the man to tend to them once we got a pen for them. If you leave another Ranger or two with me, we can run them out to graze."

"Why, Bill I never figured you for the cowboy type," Toby said. "Weston or Rowdy here sure, but I ain't never heard you go on about being a cowboy. Only Rangering."

"A man my age may well have traits and skills that you might not know anything about," Bill Retorted. "I was chasing cows long before you pups were born."

"I figure you were doing most things before any of us were born," Weston jested, chuckling. "I reckon you're as old as the hills."

"And I can still out shoot you and lick you too if I have a mind," Bill retorted. "You could no more out shoot me than you could fly."

"It looks like we are all going to do some tending to cattle," I added. "But before anything else we got to get the barn roof fixed. If some bad weather comes, we can't get the livestock under a roof if we ain't got one."

"That will be our next job, boss," Rowdy replied. "Toby, Ace, Travis and Billy Joe can get on it first thing tomorrow. Just give us a rest from riding all night, and we will be as good as new. Don't you fret about it, none. We'll have it repaired in a jiffy."

"You all ain't going to be fixing anything without lumber," I replied. "It could get costly as the hole in the roof of the barn is a big one. I figure you boy's better ride into El Paso first thing and pick up some wood and a bunch of nails. Tell them it's for me and I will tend to the bill shortly."

I was standing on the porch while Weston and Bill stepped down off of their horses. Old Bill Vents has a big smile on his mug. He has been sporting that smile pretty much all the time since we acquired the ranch.

"You know you got to have money if you intend to run this as a functioning business," Weston said. "You can't go halfway."

"And how do you propose I raise the cash?" I asked.

"You're looking right at the cash over there in the coral," Weston replied. "Selling cattle and horses from Mexico."

"You want me to sell what we just took? I ain't all that clear on us keeping the rustlers' stock as it is. What if someone suspects what we are doing?"

"Why would anybody care? You well know there ain't no way anybody is going to figure out who the beeves originally belonged to. Most ranchers on the Texan side of the border will be happy that you're doing away with the thieves."

"It seems like a glorified way to make an excuse for stealing the cattle," I implored.

"Well, what in tarnation did you plan to do with them anyway?" Bill Vents asked as he ambled over towards the edge of the porch to spit. "I don't feel the least bit bad about taking the property back from Pedro Mendez. That rascal is worse than the small-pox with his stealing and killing."

"I must agree with you, Bill," I replied. "It sure would be nice to catch Mendez and drag him back across the border."

"Wouldn't do no good," Weston responded. "The man has as many connections here in Texas as he has in Mexico. He has a ranch here and all. Even for a Texas Ranger, it would be risky to corner him. He would be out of jail in two farts anyway. A man with that much money and connections ain't going to jail and stay there for much more than a night. I reckon you would have to kill him if you want to stop him."

"It's one thing sneaking over the border to catch some horse thieves to put a bur under Mendez's blanket," I reasoned. "But to go killing important landowners in another country is an international incident and more than most folks would turn a blind eye to. Even the bosses back in Austin."

"I figure we can sell the cattle to Slim Pickens for a reasonable price," I finally agreed, giving in to the Sergeants arguments. "He'll jump at the chance of getting cheap cattle and won't have a problem with where they came from. Some of them might have originally been his anyway."

"The more rustlers we do away with, the better things will be for the local ranchers," Bill Vents assured us. "Maybe if we keep at it, we will get the attention of old Pedro Mendez, and he might lighten up on rustling Texan cattle."

"Oh I reckon we will be getting his attention in not too long," I added. "The man don't take kindly to losing livestock, although I doubt he gives a damned about the cowboys. That Mexican is more of a cash money feller."

CHAPTER 10:

DANCE HALL GIRLS

We all came back to El Paso driving the livestock ahead of us that we hadn't kept back at the ranch, and we brought the passel of rustlers with us too. After we dropped the cattle off at the stockyard, the boys and I rode the bunch of outlaws right over to Marshal Dallas Stoudenmire's jailhouse. The Marshal was there so they were promptly locked away and the judge was notified.

"Where did you pick up these cattle thieves, Ridge?" Dallas asked as he raised an eyebrow.

"We caught them down by the border," I replied.

"Why didn't you hang them then and there like you usually do?" the Marshal asked.

"I don't hang or shoot every outlaw I run into," I replied a bit taken aback. "I figure if there is a Marshal close, then it is best the local law take care of them. It works for you Dallas. You will be seen as helping to clean out the rustlers."

"I personally ain't ever seen you deliver many men to my jail, Captain."

"I only shoot those that go for their weapons or hang those that are too far away to deliver to a judge," I replied. "Which I must admit, does seem to be most of the time."

"I'll see to these rustlers, but the new judge residing in El Paso don't normally hang cattle thieves these days," the Marshal added. "He'll probably send them off to prison for seven years or so. He says it sets a better example."

"That depends on who you're setting an example for," I replied. "Most men out in West Texas ain't the reforming types. The only reason the last four rustlers surrendered was we caught them off guard. They didn't know what else to do. More often than not they start shooting as soon as they see us. Then the possibility of surrender pretty much goes right out the window. And I have a tendency to start seeing red when fired upon."

"Deputies Braggs and Hutch can take care of this lot," the Marshal stated as he nodded to his new employees. "Let's head over to Rosa's Cantina and wet our whistles."

"I'm personally in the mood for some horizontal refreshment," Sergeant Smith added.

"And when ain't you in the mood for a woman?" Bill Vents asked. "That's why you never want to be more than a Sergeant. You would have to pay too much attention to your job."

"I haven't seen you accepting any promotions!" Weston retorted.

"Would you two stop arguing for once in your lives?" I snarled as I gave my two sergeants a hard look. "There are other people here that have heard just about enough of you two hacking on each other."

This made Toby Bees and Rowdy Bates both giggle although trying not to be heard by the Sergeants. Most of the men actually enjoyed the banter between the two veteran Texas Rangers. Their pugnacious nature being the source of entertainment for the group of young lawmen. Especially when out on a boring mission. Weston and Bill were found to be more amusing than most anything else. For everyone but the Captain. Then again, he has heard the two going at it for a couple of decades.

"We left some thirty head of rustled cattle in the stockyard corral," I said to Marshal Stoudenmire. "They can try to sort them out, but most of these cattle have been stolen more than once, so the brands are modified on most of the animals. Texan ranchers ride over the border to recapture cattle stolen only to bring them back and have them rustled all over again. Nobody knows whose cattle belongs to who anymore."

"The way I see it that ain't our problem," the Marshal replied. "Our job is to capture and process the horse and cattle thieves. What is done with the livestock is none of our affairs once they're delivered. Even if they can't be delivered, you stopped the rustlers, which is our main goal. Until Pedro Mendez's men are all captured or run off, the cattle are not the issue. It's the folks stealing cattle from Texas which is our problem."

"That was the opinion of Sergeants Smith and Vents," I replied as I pondered on us taking part of the herd. "I reckon y'all are right. If it weren't for the cattle thieves, there wouldn't be any livestock to deal with."

"Clinton, you, Ace and Travis take our horses back to the Ranger post," I ordered. "Once you get done come on over to Rosa's Cantina for a bit of cold beer to clear out the trail dust from your throats."

The eight men stepped down off the jailhouse porch and headed for their favorite saloon. Kicking up dust on the dry streets of El Paso. Most of the younger Rangers pushing and shoving each other good-naturedly. All the men glad to be back in town for some fun. As we walked up to the double bat-doors both Dallas and I peered over the tops to make sure we weren't walking into trouble.

We pushed our way into the Cantina and found ourselves a table near the front door where I could keep my back to the wall. The two Sergeants, Humphrey, and the Marshal took a seat at the table with me, and the rest of the boys grabbed a couple of tables near the bar.

———

In the corner of Rosas Cantina sat a couple of men in Mexican cowboy outfits and sombreros. They had been sitting there in the corner for the best part of three days now. Waiting for the return of Captain Creek and his men. Both hombres worked for Pedro Mendez and were paid handsomely for any information that they can supply to their boss, the infamous Mexican rancher. The two spies didn't stand out as on the border there lived just as many men from

Mexico as there did from Texas and other parts of the country.

"Look at that sumbitch Captain Creek," Felipe said. "He and that Marshal aren't nothing but blowhards and bushwhackers. All puffed up with their badges. I reckon if you split the two off from the other Rangers they wouldn't be acting so tough."

"Wearing a badge and having a passel of men to back you up makes a man mighty brave," Eduardo replied. "I reckon if we killed them both Señor Mendez would give us a handsome reward."

"We were sent here to spy on them and not go at them with our guns," Felipe implored. "Anyway, I hear that Creek is mighty fast. It might not be wise to take on such a man."

"It's all stories that those Tonkawa Indians make up about that man," Eduardo retorted. "It ain't possible that a feller is as dangerous as they claim Creek is. I don't reckon there to be any Texans as hard as a Mexican when it comes to fighting or shooting. Creek has been after that Lopez for twenty years and he ain't ever been able to outsmart him or outshoot him as far as I have ever heard."

"Keep your voice down before somebody hears us, you damned fool!" Felipe whispered.

"What's the matter? Are you turning yeller on me? I ain't afraid of no Texan, no matter who he is. Be he a Marshal or a Texas Ranger."

"I ain't-a coward but I ain't plum loco either," Felipe retorted. "You keep it up with your big mouth you may well get us both killed right here. I've heard of the shootings in town between Creek and some outlaws. And Creek is still sitting there in front of us."

"I knew I should have picked somebody else to come with me instead of you," Eduardo complained.

"You didn't pick me to go with you! Señor Mendez told us both to go, you dumb bastard. And you ain't ordering me around either. Nobody made you the boss!"

"You're the one as dumb as a tree stump," Eduardo retorted. "I figure if the rest of the

Rangers leave I'm going to shoot Creek myself. I bet Mendez will give me a prize and all."

"The only prize you're going to get is a passel of lead for your troubles," Felipe said, now looking around himself to see if anybody was listening.

Both men wore un-kept scraggly mustaches on their hard dark faces and long greasy hair. They had one half-full and three empty bottles of Tequila standing before them on the round table. As they spoke, Eduardo didn't stop taking shots of tequila with lemon and salt. The hard liquor was building his confidence to a dangerous limit. Under the table, he fingered his Colt .45 revolver as he thought about the glory he would bask in if he shot and killed Captain Creek.

"If it comes to gunplay you take care of that braggart Marshal Stoudenmire," Eduardo instructed Felipe. "I can handle Creek on my own. Or are you scared of that old man of a Marshal too? Damn, I could kill him in my sleep."

As Eduardo keep fingering his revolver under the table, Felipe was sweating profusely.

Yeah, he knew that Mexican cowboys were the first to herd cattle down this way. Just like the Spanish hombre, Ponce de Leon was the very first cowboy in North America. That was originally where the Texas Longhorns came from. As scraggly an animal as they are they can withstand the harsh conditions of both north and south of the Rio Grande. But to take on city gunfighters was something that this Mexican considered to be somewhat foolish. If it hadn't been for Eduardo calling him yeller, he wouldn't have gotten involved. But, now it was a matter of honor. Even if they both ended up dead.

Eventually, the seven Texas Rangers went on along their way joined by the Sergeant they called Smith and the one-armed Ranger. Just leaving an old man with a silver star on his gun belt and three stripes on his shirt, the Marshal of El Paso and Captain Creek. Eduardo nudged Felipe when the young Rangers walked out the door, nodding his head toward the table by the double swinging doors.

Rosa's Cantina was as busy as usual that night as they had a bunch of new ladies working the floor of the saloon. Pretty much every color and race of gal was doting on the customers, urging them on to drink up so they would get their meager commission at the end of the night. Or maybe even get lucky and run into a cowhand or city dandy that was in the mood for a poke. So some more substantial earnings were in order.

"Look at that big red-haired woman with the milky white skin," Eduardo said with a look of lust on his face.

The woman standing at the bar was a tall gal by local standards. Her hair was as red as fire, and her face was peppered with freckles. What made her stand out was the provocative dress she wore that barely covered her extra-large breasts and her forward manners.

"Lookee there," Felipe said. "She just grabbed that cowboy and drug him upstairs."

"That is as forward a woman as I have ever seen," Eduardo replied. "But I sure would fancy a ride on a gal as big as her. Must be like riding a wild bronco."

"I thought that we were here to work. First, we were to spy on Captain Creek and his Texas Rangers," Felipe argued. "Then you decided all on your own that we should kill them both along with that poor old broken down man. And now you want to have a poke with that wild woman. Make up your mind on what you want to do, damn it."

"Now that you have called on me to act let's get to it then," Eduardo said as he stood to his feet, adjusting his gun belt.

Felipe followed suit knowing that this would turn out bad. And killing the old feller didn't seem right. He had a grandfather about that age. When a man gets to a certain age, he should be respected and not be forced into gunplay. Murdering innocent old fellers wasn't something that Felipe figured a man of honor did.

But Eduardo was a stupid and stubborn man at times. And if Felipe backed down now, he would be forced to leave the ranch and his job as he will have disgraced himself. So he begrudgingly followed the man his boss paired him up with. When he got back to the Mendez ranch, he had a mind to tell the boss just what happened here. That is if they live to tell the story.

Bertha shortly came back down the stairs with the cowboy with rumpled clothing. The man was still buttoning up his pants with his gun belt thrown over his shoulder running on the heels of the large Scottish woman who was moving quickly.

"I told you to stop clutching one me, you fool," Bertha snapped at the cowboy she led down the stairs.

As she made her way to the bottom another working girl walked up to her and cupped her hand over her mouth and whispered something in Bertha's ear. The big Scottish woman immediately shifted her head and eyes towards Captain Creek's table and pushed the other woman aside and moved toward the Captain, Marshal, and Sergeant.

"Captain Creek, I presume," she accused. "You were the man that let my father die at the hands of the Comanche, are you not? I saw you that day in the Indian village."

I stood to my feet and tipped my hat at the Scottish woman and said, "I saw you too but you didn't look too out of sorts with you pa trussed all up."

"On the contrary, sir," Bertha replied. "I am not at all perturbed nor was I back in the Comanche village. I came over to thank you for assisting me in gaining my freedom from that miser. If it wasn't for you, I would be in Las Cruzes now locked up in some part of the ranch house, no doubt. But without my father and brother, I am a free woman allowed to do exactly what I wish. My father's fortune is mine now, so I came here to thank you for ridding me of them both."

"I don't quite know what to say, Miss Bogardus," I replied. "I didn't kill you father although I did kill your brother Seth. He left me no choice."

"Saying you're welcome, would suffice," Bertha replied as she gave the Marshal and me a provocative smile.

Bill Vents just sat there not in the least bit surprised. Bill had been Rangering and working as a lawman for so long now that he figured he had seen just about everything there was to see. A man not easily caught off guard, although the reaction of the Captain to the Scottish girl's advances did produce a deep chuckle from the aging Ranger.

"I am sorry, Sir," Bertha added as she addressed Sergeant Vents. "I didn't see you sitting there."

"No need to excuse yourself, young lady," the old Sergeant replied. "I find that the older I get, the more often I seem to be invisible to younger folks. But I ain't done here on Earth by a long shot," he chuckled.

"So what will it be Captain Creek of the famous Texas Rangers?" Birth asked. "Are you going to allow me to give you a free poke for doing me such a favor or not?"

That proposal got another chuckle out of both the Marshal and Bill. I have always been a man who becomes uncomfortable before a forward and especially as brash a woman as was Miss Bogardus, although I had no intention to insult the Scotswoman being as I was in part responsible for the death of both her father and brother.

"I am ever so flattered that you would have an interest in a scarred up old Texas Ranger like me," I replied. "But my lady friend, Miss Zapata would most likely have something to say if I were to take you up on your kind offer. But my friend here, Marshal Stoudenmire was also responsible for stopping your brother and father in their endeavor to take over ranches and of course provide you your deserved freedom."

Bertha then turned her smiling face towards the tall gunfighter as she raised an eyebrow in question. The Marshal politely tipped his hat to the woman.

"Why I would be delighted to take you up on that offer ma-am," Dallas replied as he looked at me and winked. "I ain't married and don't have a lady friend that tells me what to do."

At that Miss Bertha Bogardus burst out laughing and grabbed the lawman's hand and nearly drug him from his chair and toward the stairs with a wicked smile on her lips.

Just then the hair on the back of my neck began to stand on end, and I got goose-bumps on my arms. Something that generally meant things are about to go sideways. I nudged Bill with my elbow, and as soon as he saw my face, he knew I was just about to see red. Pushing his chair back a bit, so he had easier access to his pistols.

"What is it you see, Ridge?" old Sergeant Bill Vents asked.

"I don't see anything yet, but I feel plenty," I replied as I scanned the room for coming violence.

————

"Now is our chance," the Mexican Eduardo whispered to Felipe. "Even that yellow-bellied Marshal is gone off with the big red-haired floozy. You kill the old man, and I'll kill Creek. It won't take more than a few seconds."

"Are you sure about this, Compadre?" Felipe asked as that bad feeling came over him again. "I ain't big on killing granddads."

"Are you going to do this with me or are you yeller?" Eduardo asked getting angry again. "I reckon that at any minute you're going to start clucking and strutting like a chicken."

But then both Mexican men stood to their feet. Figuring they would mosey over to the bar and slowly close in on the two lawmen. Catching them off guard if possible. Eduardo already had his revolver in his right hand held tight up against his hip, so it was less visible. Felipe was still puzzled on as to how he got into such a situation so quickly, but wrapped his left hand around his revolver handle just the same. His arm was now tense as he prepared to pull his weapon at the first sign of gunplay. Now that they were up and advancing toward Creek, he reckoned that it will be just as dangerous to turn and run.

As they stood at the bar, Rosa looked hard at the two men while she poured each one a shot of Tequila. She knew well enough who they were. Señor Mendez, her actual boss, had warned here that they would be here all this week but they were to spy on Creek and no more. Not to provoke a gunfight in the saloon. It seems that these two dunderheads figured they were smarter than Señor Mendez when all they are going to do is get her saloon all shot up again.

And knowing Captain Creek, probably both of the Mexican men kilt and bleeding out on her floor. Another mess to clean up.

Rosa herself had been spying on the Ranger for some time now as instructed by Mendez. Even though she was a very bright woman, he had caught her in an unhealthy financial situation and promised her if she sold him the cantina she would still be in charge and get her earnings and nobody would be the wiser. But that Mexican ranch Baron was too crafty and was continually sending other spies to watch her as well as the Texas Rangers. Now he had sent idiots like these two that were standing before her. Neither man was aware that she knew who they were. Making it impossible for her to stop what was about to happen without giving her own position away.

Just to be on the safe side, Rosa now dropped her hand behind the bar and close-up to the shelf where the eight-gauge scatter gun was kept. Ready to defend herself if the situation became unsustainable. As in such cases of extreme behavior only efficacious action is effective in stopping the violence. Rosa, knowing that impetuous want-to-be gunfighters like these two stupid cowboys will now leave us all in a tenuous situation. Men would die in the next minutes, no doubt.

It gave the Mexican inn-keeper of many years an almost eerie feeling knowing that violence was about to commence. Usually, something that happened around here with surprise and often shock. Her never being aware of something such as this before it even happened.

As she glanced at Captain Creek, she saw he was already tense. His eyes were no more than slits with his pupils sliding from one object to the other searching out the danger. Many say the man had a sixth sense. Especially the Comanche. The old Sergeant Vents was looking at Creek and speaking calmly in a whisper, but you could tell that the hard old Ranger was just as aware as Ridge was. Both men now had their hands resting on the pistol grips of their weapons. Ready to draw and fire at the slightest provocation.

To Rosa Velazquez, time seemed to stand still momentarily. Something she had heard happened in moments of extreme violence but had never seen it. She could feel a bead of sweat as it slowly rolled down the side of her face. Another drop dripped from her eyebrow into her eye making it sting. But she never took her focus off of the two gunmen and the lawmen.

Eduardo and Felipe both were looking sideways towards the two Texas Rangers through the mirror behind the bar. Rosa now had her hand on the grip of the sawed-off shotgun while she slowly pulled back one hammer and then the other. But as the room was noisy nobody heard the two metallic clicks. She noticed that she had stopped breathing such was the tension. Rosa slowly drew in a breath and intentionally controlled her fear and set her determination to save her saloon from being destroyed by these wild men of the West.

All of a sudden, the whole cantina went silent. The smell of fear was pungent in the room. Bystanders began to look for a way out. You could hear the occasional scuffling of feet but not a word was spoken such was the tension. The Captain and the old Texas Ranger Sergeant unwound their frames from their seats and stood to their feet. Now focusing on the man at the bar with his pistol in hand and the other with his hand on the handle of his Colt.

As Rosa waited and watched, she saw the Texas Ranger transform right before her. He now had blood red eyes and looked like the doctor of death himself. The veins in his neck were sticking out like rope. Apparently, a man far more dangerous than the stories told by the Indians. This was a man that had seen too much and gone too far. Past the point of no return.

The first shot fired surprised even the Mexican spies. It came from someone in the back corner of the saloon. Maybe some drunk just shooting off his gun thinking that everybody was playing. In the end, nobody ever found out who it was that fired that first round. But as soon as the gun blast rang out, all hell broke loose. It seemed that everybody drew at the same time and started shooting. Even the bystanders pulled their weapons, at least those who were armed. The rest of the folks hightailed it out of there quicker than you can spit.

So many bullets were crisscrossing the saloon numerous customers were getting killed or wounded. But others returned fire. I doubt that most of them even knew who they were shooting at. Just scared and drunk is what they were.

Captain Creek pulled his weapons so fast it was a blur. His guns were out, cocked and fire was shooting from the barrels as he put a half dozen lead slugs into Felipe and Eduardo. Neither man had time to get a shot off even with Eduardo having his gun already in hand. That was how fast Ridge Creek was. Sergeant Bill Vents also put a few bullets into the two men. But now the mayhem was contagious. Even Rosa pulled her scattergun out to shoot off her two rounds, but one of the wild bullets hit her in the right temple. Killing her dead instantly without her firing a shot.

Just about then Marshal Stoudenmire came down the staircase in red long johns firing off one revolver and then another at anybody with a gun. Excepting Ridge and Bill. Big Bertha Bogardus was moving down the stairs right behind him with a big wooden club in her grasp. Both hands clutching on the ancient Scottish weapon prepared to bash some heads in. The woman didn't even flinch at the close range gunfire.

It's a good thing that most men out West are bad shots. But at the end of the violence, six customers were dead. Rosa Velazquez, the proprietor, was found shot in the head behind the bar with the shotgun still frozen in her grasp.

And of course, the two Mexican spies, although the Texas Rangers nor the town Marshal was the wiser that these men worked for Pedro Mendez.

CHAPTER 11:

WILD BILL HICKOK

Three Texas Rangers, Marshal Stoudenmire and I all sat out on the saloon porch after the day's altercation. As the violence had passed, I had difficulty in calming down as I attempted to apply my attention to my cheroot and coffee. While I puffed the cheap cigar to life, I saw a single horse was riding down the middle of the street with a lone rider leading a mule loaded down with supplies.

"Lookee there at how that man rides his horse," Sergeant Bill Vents said. "I believe that would be Wild Bill Hickok riding into the town with the morning sun to his back. That is one cautious man."

I stood to my feet and shaded my eyes with my hand, and sure enough, it was none other than James Hickok himself.

"Howdy, James," I said as he rode up to the hitching post. "How you been hanging Pard?"

"Since when have you gone back to calling me, James?" Wild Bill asked. "You do realize that you are now in the presence of a celebrity, don't you?"

"Any man that I have seen in his long johns I don't consider a celebrity," Bill Vents said with a deep chuckle.

"You sure are in enough of those trashy dime novels of late, Pard," I added.

"I must admit, it isn't one-hundred-percent the truth. Everybody knows that scribblers are all liars. Most of them on an even keel with

Mister Vents here," the famous gunfighter said as he winked at Bill. "And that is going some."

"I beg your pardon Mister Hickok," Bill refuted taking offense. "My stories may be slightly exaggerated but never do I tell lies when I am telling tall tales."

"Why, that is a contradiction in itself, Sergeant Vents," Hickok replied with a snicker. "Tall tales are just that. If not, they would be called tall truths."

"Come on and step down off your horse, and we'll get you something to drink," I offered.

"I was thinking of some good home-style cooking from here in Rosa's Cantina," Wild Bill replied.

"I'm afraid that Rosa was shot and killed this very morning," I explained.

"It was the damnedest thing that I have ever seen, and it takes a mite for me say that," Bill Vents said. "Ridge here was the first to notice that violence was imminent. Then somebody sent a bullet sailing from the far end of the saloon, and all hell broke loose. Folks that would never pull their weapon did so and fired at will. Nobody really knows what set it off."

"Two Mexican cowboys were standing at the bar looking to make trouble," I added. "One with a gun in his hand, but they didn't start the shooting. They actually never even got a shot off before Sergeant Vents and I here gunned them down. The damnedest thing that I've ever seen."

"Well, Rosa's Cantina has always been known to have a gunfight or two upon occasion," Wild Bill replied. "What's going to happen to the saloon now?"

"The bartender is still inside working, but he don't rightly how he's going to get paid. Nobody is sure who owns the saloon now. Rosa may have some next of kin down in Mexico. But I ain't sure as I've never seen her get a visit," Marshal Stoudenmire said.

"Everybody has family somewhere," Bill Hickok replied. "It is just a matter of time before someone claims the Cantina. When money is involved relatives usually come snooping around no matter how far-flung they might be.

"That gunfight sure did leave the place shot all the hell and back," Weston observed. "And killing Rosa and all. Nobody even knows who shot her. Could have been just about anybody really."

"Bullets were flying every which way along with numerous ricochets," Bill Vents added. "She was just about to shoot off a scatter-gun into the crowd although I don't know exactly who she was aiming at. By the looks of things, it could have been us. She received a lead slug to the left temple. She was dead before she hit the floor. The woman never got one shot off. Shame to lose such a bright woman. I could hold an intelligent conversation with her which is more than I can say for you lot."

"They are still cleaning up the mess," Weston Smith stated. "I reckon it will take a few days to get new glassware and mirrors. Then fix up the broken chairs and windows."

"Must have been twenty or thirty rounds went off pretty much at the same time," I said as I cogitated on the incident. "The place has been properly ventilated."

"It's a shame I missed the excitement," Hickok replied. "I've had a long and boring ride from Flagstaff, Arizona."

"What were you doing in Arizona, Bill?" I asked. "That's a bit beyond your territory, ain't it Pard?"

"There don't exist too far to go if there is enough money in it," Hickok replied. "A man has to make a living, and it is getting more difficult all the time in my profession. A gunslinger has to follow the violence in the wilder places of the West these days."

"You could always join up with us," I said jokingly.

"You well know that I can't live on a Texas Ranger's pay," Hickok replied. "I need the finer things in life. And who would take care of all the ladies and card games if I were to be off working all the time? I prefer my periods of labor to be scattered with lots of resting, ladies and gambling time in between."

"If we want some food with our whiskey we might as well head over to the Ranger post to have Humphrey whip something up," Bill Vents said. "I doubt that the Cantina is in working order for some days to come. We sure did make a mess of the place for pretty much nothing."

"It wasn't us that started it, so we didn't actually make the mess," I replied. "Everyone in that saloon with a pistol was shooting."

"So is it true that your bosses moved you over here from Laredo all permanent like?" Bill Hickok asked. "What did you do to get sent out here where it is even wilder than East Texas?"

"I guess it being wilder is exactly why they sent me, Bill," I replied to the gunfighter. "That and my tendency to disregard what my orders are. At least when they are totally foolish. You got business out this way?"

"No, my work is done for now. I'm just passing through heading for the nearest train where I can move on back north. There is more work in Wyoming and the Dakota Territories. The towns don't have local Rangers to keep the peace. Most towns still don't even have a sheriff or marshal. Plenty of need for a good gun hand and more than enough money to pay for them. What have you been up to Ridge, other than shooting the clients in Rosa's Cantina?" Hickok asked with a smirk.

"The boss has found himself a fine woman," Bill Vents announced.

"Is that a fact?" Wild Bill asked. "I never figured you for the settling down type, Pard."

"I have never had the inclination up till now," I replied. "I even have a ranch just a few hours ride out of town. With a few head of cattle in the coral in all. Things just changed all on their own. I really wasn't looking for a woman nor a ranch. Both of them just sort of appeared at the right time and they're seeming to stick."

"I never would have thought I'd see the day," Hickok said as he looked me up and down. "Not that it's a bad thing. Our way of life has its risks, and hazards now don't it? Never knowing where you're going to lay your head down. Or who you will have to kill next. Or maybe get killed yourself. As you well know, sometimes you get, and sometimes you get got."

As they arrived at the post, Humphrey went about fixing up some steak cuts, baked potatoes, corn on the cob, black beans, and rice. Serving the men sitting in the Ranger mess hall.

"What happened to all the chairs?" Bill observed.

"They have been confiscated by the men and moved to the porch where we spend most our idle time here at the post," I replied. "Although of late that there ain't been all that much time off actually."

After the meal, the men headed off for a drink in the Wig-Wam Hotel and Saloon. A good walk as the Ranger post was at the edge of town and the red-light district was on the opposite side. So the men enjoyed the stroll, smoking and talking about times past.

"We usually split up our leisure time between Rosa's Cantina, the Black Water Saloon, and the Red Light Bar," I said. "If I remember right the Red Light is your favorite gambling spot, ain't it Wild Bill?"

"I lost too much money there on my last visit. After you boys took off back to Laredo I stayed on a spell and lost all the earnings I made killing those outlaws. I reckon the quality of poker game is not so high at the Wig-Wam when compared to those card cheating city slickers in the Red Light Bar."

So we ventured over the Wig Wam Hotel and Saloon. Several card games were going on at various tables in the room. We took a table while Bill observed the action in the poker games, deciding which table he would take a seat at. A bottle of whiskey was produced by the bartender, and each of the men nursed their whiskeys while Bill kept an eye on the cards.

"Playing cards is like an art to which some become addicted," Bill said as he focused on the dealers at each table. "Once you start it is seldom that a man can stop. It's that feeling of being lucky at some particular point when you find it impossible to resist another game. Just knowing that today is the day that you're going to bust the bank."

"I've seen you play cards a passel of times and I ain't never seen anything happen but the bank busting you, Wild Bill," Sergeant Vents snickered.

"Yeah well, I'm afraid that although I do love the game, I really ain't worth a damn at playing," Bill replied with a small smile. "Even when I do win I usually continue to play until I lose what I just won. That table near us looks like it has the dumbest looking players. The dealer looks bored too so I might have a chance there."

"Let's have another drink while you continue to cogitate on the matter," Vents said. "I reckon the best decision you could make now was not to play at all. You're only going to lose anyway."

With that James Butler Wild Bill Hickok stood to his feet, adjusted his revolvers and sauntered over to the table with the lesser skilled opponents.

"Deal me in my good sir," Bill said with a smile. "I have that feeling that luck is about to visit."

The dealer had not been paying all that much attention to the game. But when Wild Bill Hickok pulled up a chair and took a seat his demeanor changed. Now the man's eyes were sharp as the cards appeared to be no more than a blur of motion with the professional dealer shuffling them. Passing the deck to the man on his left to cut. The house dealer quickly began to send each card sailing across the table and over the money in the kitty. Finally landing after twirling across the green felt. Stopping in front of the hands of each player at the table.

"Hickok!" A man in the street yelled out. "I know you're in there you bushwhacking bastard. I come here to kill you. I've been trailing you ever since you left Arizona you murdering scum. I plan to send you straight off to Hell, Wild Bill!"

"It looks like you gentlemen will have to excuse me for a brief moment," Wild Bill politely stated and he had a last look at his hand of cards which he saw were three aces and a pair of deuces. "Anybody has a look at those cards while I'm away, Marshal you shoot them for me."

Bill was indeed a tall man as he unfolded himself from his seat. He stood out even more due to the fancy long-coat and red sash he wore. Sort of like teasing folks about who he was, leaving no one to mistake him for another. Yeah, Hickok was about as original as a man can get. The women loved him even more than the men. And I mean all of them. Married or not. I always said that if Bill died young, it would be from the bullet of a jealous husband.

"Would you like to be my second, Ridge?" Bill asked me almost formally.

"Sure enough, Pard," I replied as I stood to my feel adjusting my pistols till they felt comfortable.

"It's always nice to be sure there ain't some bushwhacking sons of bitches hiding in an alley or shadow to give the challenger an advantage. Especially with you carrying those two cannons you got today."

"I'm toting my city guns," I replied. "Peacemakers with the gun sights filed down as sharp as a razor. Best to draw some blood if you have to hit an outlaw in town. With what happened yesterday I aim to try to club the victims before the shooting starts. The folks around El Paso have too much a tendency to start firing and ask questions later."

As the two tall gunslingers crossed the bar and began to make their way out of the Wig

Wam Saloon doors, in came a big red-haired woman moving at a fierce pace.

"Excuse me, gentlemen," she said as she moved us aside and headed in through the bat-wing doors. "I'm looking for a new job. There's no more work to be had at Rosa's Cantina after you shot it to pieces."

As the woman pushed us both clear, Bill had a look at the large floozy and raised an eyebrow in question.

"You don't even want to know, Bill," I replied to his look. "She is the daughter of the old Scottish Lord and his son that we had to kill just recently."

"And you claim that you're settling down? To me, it looks like you are cleaning out the general population of West Texas. I'd swear you're getting worse than me. And I thought that I was a magnet for trouble. Amigo, you are the trouble!"

"Be that as it may, who would you rather have your back today?" I asked with a snicker. "Me or some huckleberry?"

Wild Bill Hickok & El Paso's Red Light Saloon

Wild Bill Hickok, Texas Jack & Buffalo Bill Cody

"Oh, there is no doubt that you are the best backup that money can buy, or as in our case friendship can buy," Bill replied. "But you must admit that at times it is hard to stop you once you start. It seems that only Sergeant Smith has some certain amount of luck in that matter. I myself have never ventured to cause you to divagate from your chosen course of action as I don't wish to endanger my life needlessly."

"Don't you worry now, Bill," I replied with a grin. "I may shoot just about everybody else in sight, but I reckon with you wearing that red sash around your waist like some dandy I'll most likely recognize you before I pull the trigger."

"You know that I like a little flamboyance in my dress," Wild Bill replied with a smile. "I do have a bit of the showman in me. Even had a go at some Wild West Show with Bill Cody but although I dress the part, I can't act for shit."

As we passed through the doors and across the porch, sure enough, a man was standing by his horse tied to the hitching rail waiting ready to draw on the gunslinger.

"Who the hell are you?" Bill Hickok asked the challenger. "I like to know who it is I'm going to shoot."

"You killed my brother back in Arizona," he replied. "And now I'm here to kill you, Bill."

"The name is Mister Hickok to you, sir," Bill replied in rebuttal. "And I have killed a bunch of men in Arizona, so I am afraid that you are going to have to be more specific."

I had a look around the street and saw one man out of the corner of my eye that seemed out of place. Sort of hiding in the first shadow of the alley. His revolver was in his holster, but his hand was gripping the handle so tight his knuckles were white.

I quickly moved down the side of the building so I could sneak up on the feller hiding in the shadows without him noticing. As soon as I got up behind him, I quietly pulled my long Peacemaker revolver and gave the man a solid thump in the head making sure that the sharp gun sight made a cut down the side of the man's face. When he comes around covered in his own blood his bravery should have been cut down a notch or two. As Wild Bill heard the thump, he glanced his eyes my way slightly nodding his head.

"Now your bushwhacking partner is out of commission, mister," Bill informed the man. "Are you sure you still want to go through with this? Even if you do shoot me that Texas Ranger over there is going to kill you dead. It don't have to end up that way. You just drop your gun and Captain Creek over there, and I will take you to the Marshals office to stand trial."

"I ain't done nothing illegal, yet!" the man retorted.

"But indeed you have, sir," Wild Bill informed the man. "Intending harm to officers of the law is a serious offense. Me, as I am an appointed and bonded Territorial Marshal and the Captain because he is a Texas Ranger. You have but two choices now. Draw or go to jail. But I'll warn you now. You make me pull on you, and I'll put you down."

"I didn't come here to talk Hickok," the unknown man replied. "I came here to kill you for what you have done to my brother."

Bill just stood there with his hands on the white carved handles of his Navy Colts. A gash of a mouth set at an angle with his eyes flashing danger at the challenger. Then everything went into slow motion as it does at times of violence. All sound dropped away from the men about to tempt fate with the pull of a gun and a piece of flying lead.

The unknown gunman shifted his weight right before he drew his Colt .45. Something that experienced city gunfighters knew happened just before a country gunfighter went for his pistol. Giving Hickok a good edge on the man while pulling both of his revolvers and pulling both triggers at the same time.

The man's gun was in his hand and on the rise when the two lead slugs hit him in the right and left sides of his chest. Making his eyes go a milky white with a blank expression just before he dropped to the ground.

Hickok walked up to the feller and looked deep into his fading eyes, his two Colts still pointing at the aggressor.

"Who the hell were you anyway?" Hickok asked.

But the man just mouthed words as red bubbles formed at his lips. A gurgling sound was coming from the man's lungs. The same bubbles came popping out of the two holes in his chest. Both lungs punctured and damaged beyond repair.

I walked up beside Bill but when I arrived the man had already passed. Marshal Stoudenmire came from the saloon door where he had observed the entire incident. As he reached the body, he looked through the man's pockets but only found a plug of tobacco and a picture of a smiling woman. That and a few coins.

"He ain't even carrying enough damned money to pay for his burial," the Marshal complained. "Not a document one on the man, so we have no idea who he is unless your memory freshens up some, Wild Bill."

"Since he didn't give me a name nor do I recognize his face he could be just about anybody, Dallas. And who is watching my cards?" Bill asked.

"I'll have the gravedigger come by with the wheelbarrow and cart him off," the Marshal said.

"He'll have to wait for a spell in the smokehouse as I don't think that they've finished burying the folks killed in Rosa's Cantina just yet. But I reckon he won't mind the wait now."

CHAPTER 12:

CAPTAIN ROWDY BATES

Rowdy Bates and Travis Picket rode out of the Ranger post, heading toward Laredo. All the way across southern Texas. As expected Tuc and Potak were waiting just outside of town to escort the two Rangers along the trail to San Antonio and finally down to Laredo. The two Tonkawa Indians were sitting beside the road in the shade of their horses. Both men were sitting on top of a small blanket with their legs crossed.

"Why, howdy Tuc, Potak," Rowdy Bates said. "You boys ready to head home?"

"We're always at home," Tuc replied.

"When we get back to Laredo we will return to El Paso to work for Captain Creek," Potak informed the two men. "Toby Bees will stay with the Captain and we will too."

"I was kind of hoping that you two would hang around for a while to help out till I get used to being in charge," Rowdy replied.

"You know more than enough to be a Captain, Rowdy. You have been ready for some time now. You just didn't know it," Potak said. "We have been with the Captain for many summers and winters and we are too old for change."

"Well, alright then," the new Captain Bates said, wondering who it was he was going to be ordering around.

Only a few men were left back at the Laredo Ranger post and the best one there was Frances Cooks. Dudley Spurs and Gus Gavin were good men too. Of course, Travis was going to be his

Sergeant. He doesn't know it yet, but he is the next best man available. When Rowdy and Travis return to the post, there will be precisely thirteen Rangers back in the Laredo. A number that made the new Captain uneasy being such a superstitious man and all. A least there was some veteran material to work with. And according to Captain Creek, there are more recruits headed for Laredo from Austin.

The unknown factor of the near future for the new Captain wasn't crossing all of Texas again. It was what state of affairs the post would be in when they arrived. They all had been gone for a good spell now, although Cooks was left in charge, so Rowdy didn't expect things to be too bad. Frances had been with the Captain for a long time and had seen a good number of battles. But Rowdy doubted that he had organized any missions, so he wasn't expecting the men to be as sharp as they have to be to hunt outlaws. He reckoned that he had some work to do with the men before they ventured out to fight Comanche again.

As they passed Van Horn, Tuc and Potak disappeared. Rowdy had been around those two for so long that he hardly noticed when the appeared or vanished. Knowing that they were close enough to come running if things went sideways. But Travis wasn't so confident and didn't like riding across the Comanche Trail with it being just him and Rowdy.

"It's kind of spooky out here all on our own," Travis said.

"Most folks spend their entire life worrying about one thing or another that never happens," Rowdy replied. "And if it does, you can't stop it anyway, so there ain't no use pondering on it so."

"I ain't feeling too lucky on this trip."

"Luck don't even work like that you fool," Rowdy retorted. "Luck is something that you can control if you know the signs to avoid."

"Have you seen any signs of bad luck up to now, Captain?"

Rowdy noted the change from Travis using his name to using his new rank. This made the Texas Ranger Captain puff up his chest a bit and boosted his confidence.

"Don't you fret none," Rowdy replied. "If trouble comes our way I assure you we will handle it. Be it stand and fight or high tail it out of here. We are good shots with our pistols and rifles, we have fast horses, and the Tonkawa are out there somewhere keeping an eye on things. If some bad folks show, Tuc and Potak will see them well before we do."

Captain Rowdy Bates was, in fact, a confident man. Yeah, he did have his quirky ways with his superstitious streak and all, but the man was damned fast with a gun and didn't miss once he took a bead on an outlaw or hostile for that matter. He had no hesitation in taking over the Ranger post although he still didn't know how the men back in Laredo will react to his being made Captain. That will be something that time will tell, and Captain Bates will probably have to prove his worth before he wins the respect of all of the men.

"I figure that if we ride hard, we can cover sixty miles or so a day. That leaves San Antonio just over some five-hundred miles away. Maybe some ten days or so. Then it is about the same distance ride down to Laredo. Figure some twenty days to cross the state."

The men had two extra horses each so they wouldn't wear out their mounts. Plus they planned to stop in San Antonio for a day or two rest and to visit the local saloons.

Rowdy Bates was wondering what Fannie Porter would think of him making Captain so quick and all. He reckoned with his new rank the women folk would now fall at his feet. Not that Rowdy Bates ever had much trouble getting to know the ladies. With his wavy hair combed back and his blue eyes, the tall Ranger made most of the women he met turn their heads for a second look. The man's apparent confidence made him stand apart from most men. Something that was much more noticeable when he was not with Captain Creek. A man who stole the thunder from pretty much anybody that rode with him.

CHAPTER 13:

FORT GRAVEYARD

Festus Willis had been kicking around Texas for some time now. He was a Sheriff up in the Texas Hill Country when he had been noticed by Pedro Mendez. Pedro had small ranches all across the state where he hid out his rustled cattle. Keeping his activities hard to track to any observers. The Mexican ranch baron had started working on bringing Festus Willis into his fold the day they met. Not that it was any problematic feat bribing Festus.

A man of questionable honor from the get-go. But that is precisely the kind of man that Mendez was looking for. A Texan lawman with a dark if not dubious past. Making him the perfect target to tend to the crafty old Mexican's dirty deeds. A man who valued money over his morals and any standards that society set. Even with him being a Sheriff in all.

It wasn't really all that unusual for a gunman or possibly even a wanted man to become a Sheriff. The lawmen in such wild country as the West had to be hard gun hands so many may have committed a crime in one state only to become a Sheriff in another, much like Festus Willis.

Old Pedro Mendez had sent word back east to have the detective agency of one Scottish born Allan Pinkerton to check on the past of Mister Festus Willis and found that he had been said to have committed the odd murder. He had fought in the Civil War after running from the law back east. When he mustered out of the Union Army, he bounced around from one wild cow town to another until he came across Fort Graveyard. The city had no law at all at that time, and it never had any law in the past. Thus the name, as the graveyard had as many inhabitants as the folks living above ground in this town. Of course, it had not always been called Fort Graveyard. At one time it had been merely Fort Brimstone. A small forgotten out of the way Army post during the war. Now just the remnants of a town with a countryside full of small ranches.

Pedro Mendez dreamed of driving enough herds of rustled livestock up here to the Hill Country and maybe take a few thousand head of cattle all the way to Abilene. Each head of beef was worth four dollars down by the Mexican border, but the same animal was worth forty dollars when delivered as far as the Abilene train station. The beeves were then shipped back east where they brought even more money. Pedro Mendez figured he could make a fortune.

Not that the man had any idea of just how much land he owned and how many head of cattle he possessed on any particular day. But he was another one of these men that are only satisfied when they have everything they see. Regardless of the price which is to be paid.

Well, once Festus was bribed and working for Pedro he began to receive a handsome salary and quickly became accustomed to a high lifestyle. Plenty of poker, whiskey, and visits to the pleasure palace for Mister Willis. So when the Mexican rancher proposed that he go work for the Texas Rangers in Austin for a substantial increase in pay, the Sheriff was far too greedy to turn the offer down. Even though it meant that the Sheriff would no longer be allowed to take the liberties he did there in Fort Graveyard. At least for the time being, obliged to act like a Texas Ranger. So off he went to Austin where Pedro had already had him enlisted as a Corporal due to his time in the Union Army.

With Mendez having greased the palms of two of the higher ranking officers of the Austin office of the Texas Rangers, Willis was soon to become a trusted member of the group of lawmen. And shortly his transfer papers were submitted, and he would be moved from the central offices to El Paso to serve under Captain Ridge Creek and Sergeants Vents and Smith. He would remain as Corporal so as not to create any conflicts with Creeks best and longest-serving men. The plan had been worked out carefully and now, along with a half-dozen other

Ranger recruits he was sent to the far western borders of Texas with New Mexico. Corporal Willis was to lead this patrol of new men meant to cross the state to get to their new posting.

The seven Rangers rode out of Austin in the early morning, just before first light. The Corporal was at the head of the single file of Rangers. The ex-sheriff pushed the new men hard just for the enjoyment. Festus himself having a mean streak in him a mile wide. Something that up till now he had been able to hide from his commanding officers back in Austin. But on his own, he made life as hard as he could for the young recruits.

"Get your lazy asses moving, or I am going to make you all walk!" Willis yelled. "I intend to cover eighty miles today and if we don't do it with daylight I indent to ride tonight until we do. I'll teach you pups to go joining the Texas Rangers."

"We're doing the best we can," Ranger Dakota Brock replied as he tried to catch his breath.

"Well, that ain't good enough, Ranger!" Corporal Willis refuted.

"But we're dying out here at this pace," the Ranger pup replied.

"Dying ain't much of a living, boy," Festus said as he put the spurs to his horse.

The small patrol of Rangers rode on into the twilight but finally stopped for some rest. Festus really stopped for the horses as he didn't give a damn what happened to these greenhorns.

"Blue Bonnet Sparks" the Corporal called out. "You take the first turn at guard with two-hour shifts. Dan Kelly will spot your turn, and the last shift goes to Calhoun Snider. If I catch one of you three asleep during your watch, I shoot you myself, and that is not a threat. It's a promise."

"Yes Sir, Corporal Willis," Blue Bonnet replied.

"Where in the world did you get the name Blue Bonnet, you mutt?" the Corporal asked. "It's the stupidest name I have ever heard of."

"How would I know why my folks named me Blue Bonnet? They were killed when I was just a boy. Why are you riding us so hard Corporal?"

"You already did two things wrong!" Willis retorted. "One is you asked me a question, and two is you asked me another question. Don't speak unless you're spoken to or asked something. Then answer the question and not another word. Now which one of you sorry excuses for lawmen knows how to cook? And that is a question!"

"I've cooked some back home for my pa," Dakota Brock replied before he realized he even spoke up.

"Then unpack the mule and get some supper going. I'm hungry, and it puts me in a foul mood. So move your asses. The rest of you boys tend to the horses. Get your tail moving dough boxer, or I'll be having you for supper."

After about a week on the trail, right around Sonora, Festus Willis started to get the feeling that they were being watched. But he couldn't see anything out of the ordinary. Just the same, the man kept looking over his shoulder all the time. As if he was expecting to see a Comanche war party at any moment. Something that didn't go unnoticed by the younger Ranger recruits. Each and every one getting more nervous by the minute.

They rode all through that day with a foreboding feeling. Knowing that they were about halfway to El Paso, so there was nowhere close to take cover. They pushed on through the afternoon. Now Corporal Festus Willis didn't have to tell the boys to press their mounts. Most of the day they were nearly overtaking the Corporal. They rode until the sun just started to set on the horizon. Making sure that they had time to find some high ground for the night. There was no need to place guards tonight as not one of the men got a wink of sleep. At least not until nearly first light.

As the night waned and a slight glow showed on the heavens to the east, they all fell asleep at pretty much the same time and without putting out even one guard. It was a serious oversight by the Corporal of the Ranger patrol.

Festus Willis suddenly opened his eyes, and he found himself with a large Bowie knife at this throat. He could feel a warm rivulet of blood run down the side of his neck. He was looking into the eyes of the most frightful Indian he had seen in his entire life. A man with a gash of a mouth sporting a wicked smile.

"What are you all doing out here with no guards posted?" Tuc asked Willis.

Tuc released the pressure of the blade from the ex-sheriff's neck and Festus immediately started kicking backward out of reach of the Tonkawa Indian, raising dust as he moved back. He reached for his gun to shoot but his holster was empty.

"You looking for this?" Potak snickered. "You boys sure are sorry excuses for Texas Rangers. The two of us could have killed all seven of you and stole your horses, and you wouldn't have even woken up."

"Who the hell do you think you are?" Willis said trying to put on a brave show for the other Rangers who were now all awake.

"We are scouts for Captain Creek," Tuc replied, still looking like he wanted to carve Willis up. "I know you men are Rangers but what are you all doing out here acting a fool?"

"Who you calling a fool you redskin?" Willis retorted as he pulled out his Bowie knife.

Potak aimed the Corporal's own pistol at him and snickered, "Never bring a knife to a gunfight, boy."

Much to the dismay of Corporal Willis his men also got a chuckle out of this. The ornery man who had been making their life miserable was getting his own at the hands of these two frightening Indians. Especial the one with the scalps sewn to his buckskins.

"We will be staying here until the other Texas Rangers arrive," Potak instructed. "It will be shortly."

"I ain't accustomed to having Indians telling me what to do," Festus Willis complained. "Who the hell do you think you are?"

"We know who we are," Tuc replied with that evil grin of his as he pointed a pistol at Willis. "What we have to find out is who are you?"

Tuc stood there keeping an eye on this shifty Corporal and the rest of the men as Potak went back and retrieved their horses where they had them hidden. Then the two men sat down on the dusty earth and watched as the sun rose on the eastern side of their world. Both men looking like it was something that they had not expected to see again. Gazing at the incredible sight as if it had a unique value that the white men didn't understand.

As the nine men sat beside the road about an hour after sunrise Rowdy Bates came riding up to the unannounced Ranger patrol.

"Hey Potak," Rowdy said as he rode up to the group of men. "Where in the dickens did you find all these Ranger pups? What are you boys doing all the way out here?"

"They were fixing to get kilt," Tuc replied. "No guards out at night in Comanche Territory. Your Corporal here ain't all that careful as he should be."

"Is that true, Corporal?" Rowdy asked.

"I'm Corporal Festus Willis of the Texas Rangers headquarters," the ex-sheriff retorted as if mentioning the head office would put some fear into Rowdy.

"What are you? Another Austin pencil pusher like most of those men that give us stupid orders. Hell, the main Ranger office is a long ways away when you are out here in the wild country. You have not left me impressed mister. And how in the world do you figure you all will survive if you don't put guards out at night? We have a good moon now, and this is just when the Comanche make their raiding parties."

"And who the hell are you to be talking to me in such a manner?" Willis retorted. "I'm in charge of this patrol and not you."

"And since when does a Corporal outrank a Captain?" Rowdy asked with a smile on his face as he opened and closed his gun hand. "I am Captain Bates out of Laredo. It is my business if you are out here with a bunch of Ranger recruits acting a fool. These men look as green as can be."

"I have orders to deliver the bunch of recruits to Captain Creek in order to fill out the El Paso Ranger force with more men and another officer," Willis stated.

"Let's see those orders, Corporal," Captain Bates ordered, clearly not liking Willis. "Come on, I ain't got all day."

After Bates read the orders, he handed them back to the Corporal. The Ranger recruits were now nervous as the Tonkawa Indians looked as fierce as can be and even the other Texas Rangers seemed unfriendly.

"You best tend to these men better, or Captain Creek will serve your nuts to the squirrels. He is not as patient a man as I am."

"You better stop riding those horses so hard, or you won't make it to El Paso without losing one or more," Potak said as he eyed the state of the animals in the Corporal's patrol. "If you get set afoot out here you will perish."

Then the two Texas Rangers along with Tuc and Potak turned their horses east again and rode off without another word.

"There's something I don't like about that Willis feller," Rowdy said to Travis as they were moving eastbound again.

"He seemed alright enough to me," Travis replied.

"Your problem is that you're too affable, Ranger Picket. Trust men sparingly if you intend to survive. Even if they seem to be on the same side. I judge a man by his actions and not by a beige hat, a silver star and a couple of pistols."

"I reckon the best way to give a man a chance is to do just that. Give him a chance," Travis replied.

"The best way to give a man a chance to show his true colors is not to trust him until he proves himself worthy," Tuc added. "He could kill you before he proves himself to be honest."

CHAPTER 14:

RANCH LIFE

Ridge Creek had taken more and more to spending time on the Windy Ridge Ranch with Lola Zapata. A lifestyle that he was effortlessly sliding into.

It seems that as long as the Captain stays out here on the Ranch, he never runs into much trouble. But as soon as he goes into El Paso, there is usually some violence to tend to. As

Lola pondered on the possibilities of her settling down with Ridge she looked out across the small pond and creek to the surrounding hills. It was indeed a quiet lifestyle when compared to living in the busy cities of El Paso and Paso del North in Mexico where her father had his other store. A business that Lola was in charge of but now seldom visited.

At the moment her focus was on Captain Ridge Creek. At the first sight of this battle scared man Lola had been love struck. With his rock-solid confidence and rugged but handsome features. That and especially the fact that this famous and fearless Texas Ranger Captain constantly stumbled over his feet and words every time he was with Lola. A sure fired sign that he too was just a smitten with her as she was with him.

It joyed the woman when she could take such a confident man and render him speechless. But then again Lola had a sharp and witty tongue. She had always been famous for leaving her suitors speechless. Perhaps that was the reason that she never did get serious with any of the men that attempted to court her.

Most men didn't understand her ways and gave up after the first rebuttal or two.

But Ridge was different. No matter how much Lola made fun of him, he wouldn't give up. He just stood up to the bright Mexican woman's endless poking fun at him. Something that she doubted very much that anybody else had attempted. Surely not another man. But Lola also knew when to stop with her hacking on a man. She knew when it was time to be tender and not speak so defiantly. Yes, she believed that she had won this Texas Ranger over lock stock and barrel.

At the moment the Captain was out on patrol with his men looking for more cattle rustlers. But she wasn't alone here on the Ranch. Sergeant Bill Vents was also staying on as he rode out on less and less missions as the aging Ranger also became fond of the Windy Ridge Ranch. Old Bill also tended to Lola's every need. He cooked for her and took her on rides. She, in turn, helped him tend to the horses and take the cattle out to the different pastures to graze.

Little by little the ranch had acquired a more substantial amount of livestock. With every trip south of the border Captain Creek would cut out half the stock they confiscated and add it to his herd. They had sold some of the cattle off to repair the massive hole in the barn's roof making it a good place to keep the animals in foul weather. That and stockpile a little cash for a rainy day. There were even a couple of cowboys that came over to the Windy Ridge Ranch to help Bill out. They came from Slim Pickens Double HH spread. Just enough assistance to keep Bill and the chores all up to date. And of course, Lola helped out wherever she could. The woman caught on fast when it came to cows and was already skillful on her horse and a fair shot with her pistol.

As she stood at the edge of the ranch house porch, Bill Vents came up behind her.

"How about a baked apple with cinnamon and honey, Miss Lola?" Bill asked as he came out with a tray and two baked apples and two cups of Texan coffee.

"Did you add some milk to my coffee to water it down a tad?" Lola asked Bill.

"Oh, yes ma-am," Bill replied. "I know you don't like your coffee as strong as we drink it.

Now eat your apple before it gets cold, or it won't be as tasty."

Bill grabbed a chair and had a seat as he munched on his fruit and sipped his beverage. Lola did likewise and ate her sweet apple in silence. Only the sound of the livestock was auditable. That and the constant breeze that blew over the top of the ridge. Keeping the Texan heat at bay during the day.

The ranch house itself was built of thick adobe walls which kept the interior cool during the day and warm at night. Lola had already been busy installing curtains on all of the windows and a few niceties that she brought from the general store her father owned. Making the home cozier although Ridge had complained some about the curtains. Something he saw to be a waste of money. And he said just as much.

"Windows are there to look out of," he had argued. "And at night once you blow out the kerosene lanterns nobody can see in. It just don't make no sense to put curtains up way out here on the ranch."

But Bill Vents thought that the additions made the building feel more like folks lived there. Not just some range shack that was used when tending to the horses and cattle. Bill Vents had made his permanent quarters in the bunkhouse. Selecting the best bunk right by a window so he could see the sun come up of a morning. And most every evening old Bill would build a fire just off to the side of the porch where he had drug several logs to sit on. A place for Bill to spin yarns of his years with Captain Creek and the Texas Rangers.

That night Lola, Bill, and the two cowhands were sitting around the fire talking about one thing and another that should be done on the ranch. A bigger fenced in area to hold the new cattle that were brought in. The need to cut out the best stock for sale in the El Paso market to keep raising funds to cover the costs of running a small ranch.

"Do you think that Ridge will ever really settle down here on the ranch with me, Bill," Lola asked. "Every time I think he is going to stay here for a couple of weeks he up and rides off to tend to some other mission or other."

"To be honest, I am surprised that you have managed to tame him down enough that he spends several days at a time here on the ranch. You are the first woman that I have ever seen to have such an influence on the Captain," Bill replied in all seriousness. "He is, in fact, a changed man. So, the answer to your question is probably. Of course with Ridge, there is nothing one-hundred-per-cent certain as he has lived pretty much all his life running from one battle or another. But just the fact that with you he stays on at times for a whole week just goes to show you that he is changing his perspective on home life."

"I could do with him adapting a little faster than he is," Lola replied. "Women are not as patient as men make us out to be. Especially when it comes to my man and getting hitched."

"Hitched?" Bill asked, somewhat taken aback. "You really think that you can get Ridge to get hitched?"

"Well, I'm not fixing up the ranch house so you'll be more comfortable you old fool!" Lola said, but with a smile on her lips.

"I reckon I never cogitated on the Captain getting hitched and settling down," Bill said with a thoughtful expression. "It is indeed a rare thing when someone surprises me. But, ma-am you come up with surprises, one right after another."

"Well you can start pondering on it now as that is what I intend to do," Lola stated in that confident and brash tone of hers. "If Ridge doesn't settle down now he won't ever settle down. It's time for us to have a couple of brats to run around the house and all."

"Ridge Creek a pa?" Bill asked incredulously. "I'm sorry Miss Lola, but you are going a mite too fast for me."

She put her fists on her hips and leaned back as she laughed. The woman thoroughly enjoyed leaving men off balance. Something that she did seem to be an expert at.

"Have you told all this to Ridge?" Sergeant Bill Vents asked as he sat there with his mouth open.

"If you don't close your gob a bird just might fly right in," she added to Bill's discomfort.

Windy Ridge Ranch Hand & El Paso, Texas (1860's)

"Now get off that lazy old butt of yours and let's get to work."

The bossy but somehow utterly charming Miss Lola had Bill running about the house fixing everything that they could find that was broken or just about to fall apart.

"Those two windows don't open either," Lola added as she took a crowbar and put it between the window seal and the window frame. Wrenching the window open from which a gentle breeze immediately came in.

"Now look at that," she stated. "Some of the fixing-up here just makes it nicer in the house. Now let's get at that stove. It looks like it may have never had a good cleaning."

CHAPTER 15:

SOUTH OF THE BORDER

My Texas Rangers and I rode over the Rio Grande once again in search of rustlers and cattle. This is something that has become a habit. First of all, it was much more effective. Even though we have caught more than a half dozen rustler gangs with cattle and horses in the last weeks, they still seem to keep on trying to steal the cattle despite our efforts. We had been going out once or twice a week. Riding south just after sunset and returning just before sunrise.

We had been on a lucky streak and caught a herd and a half dozen rustlers every time we went out. It was working like a clock. Old Pedro Mendez must be moving a herd or two just about every night. What surprised me so much was that he knew we were making raids south of the river but it didn't seem to deter Pedro's plans in the least bit. Even though every rustler we caught ended up in prison with a stiff sentence or was hung by the neck until dead.

We had once again ridden south with my veteran Rangers. The new recruits had arrived in El Paso along with Corporal Willis, but their metal was yet to be tested. And I was not generous with my plans when they include possible international incidents. Especially for Rangers that I have no way to check on their backgrounds and have not ridden into a battle with one of the Sergeants or me yet.

So for the moment the new recruits and Corporal Festus Willis were restricted to the Ranger Post, and I had left Clinton Westwood in charge of the lot. Clinton was not my best man on the trail, but at the post, he seemed to understand my orders and follow them to the letter. The Rangers biggest problem was him falling asleep while on patrol. The man slept in the saddle just about as well as he slept in his bunk back at the barracks.

Clinton Westwood always said, "I never walk when I can ride and never stand when I can sit."

When I put Clinton in charge of the post until my return, Willis had plenty to say as he was sent to El Paso to work as a Corporal. But I was getting mixed feelings from this man. And Tuc and Potak said that they nor Rowdy Bates liked him from the get-go. Catching the drop on the Ranger in the middle of the Austin to El Paso trail. If the Tonkawa had been Comanche, we would have never heard from those boys again.

Keeping this incident in mind, I decided that I would not trust Corporal Willis with any of my men until he had proved his commanding skills and I see that the men take well to him. Nobody is running a contest to see who the most popular officer is, nor are we too soft on the new men. But if the men don't like their Captain, Sergeant or even Corporal there's less chance that they will listen to him when the time comes for violence. Over the years I have also heard of the odd case of a Corporal or Sergeant getting shot by his own Rangers for sending them out on a stupidly planned mission. I hate stupid people.

I have in the past been sent on what I considered poorly planned patrols. Even while I was under Captain RIP Ford. But as I look back at it now, I can see why the man did what he did. Often wisdom is not immediately understood. But stupidity is a trait that is difficult to hide.

And Willis seemed to be a tad too far on the dumb side to lead my men into battle. A stupid man who thinks he knows everything and at the same time he is oblivious to his own ignorance. The most dangerous kind of stupid as far as I'm concerned. It puts me in mind of several men I have met in the past. Each and every one thinking that they knew more and better than everyone else when they actually didn't have any idea of what they are doing. I have always thought that confidence is the feeling you have before you understand the situation you are in.

Like most nights we all pulled up and dismounted sitting on the ground waiting for Tuc and Potak to come back with information on the location of tonight's rustlers. So far, we had gotten the drop on the outlaws that we have caught up till now. Tuck and Potak move from one moon shadow to another and are rarely seen when they don't intend to be. So they seek out the outlaws checking their tracks to make sure they are coming from Texas. They then return to us and give us the exact location of their herd and the direction they are riding in.

As herding cattle is a slow process under most conditions, we have plenty of time to ride around and get ahead of them. Setting up an ambush as they head our way. Then we gather up the bunch and head then back north. Me keeping the better part of the cattle and a few horses, as they were stolen on more than one occasion anyway. And running the rest of the animals to El Paso and into holding pens in the stockyards. Then the outlaws that don't get shot and die go to trial to test their luck.

We waited for the Tonkawa for about two hours before they came back and advised us that a good-sized herd of cattle was heading our way right from the Rio Grande just north of us. So we didn't even have to move. There were fourteen of us counting Tuc and Potak. I sent five men along with Toby Bees to wait on the outlaw's right flank and five men along with

Weston to sit over here on their left flank. Then I rode down the trail a bit where we planned to stop the cattle. It looked pretty much like it had ever other night we had ridden out in the last weeks.

But this time something spooked the rustlers and just before they came by our position they started to shoot off their pistols and stampede the horses and cattle south. The problem with stampedes is the cattle often don't go in the direction that they are planned to. In the end, the bunch ran back north to where they came from, but the outlaws spurred their horses south to escape what they now knew to be a trap.

When they rode past Weston's and Toby's men, everybody started firing their rifles at the Mexican rustlers. And the rustlers were shooting off their revolvers at us Texas Rangers. All of them knew if they killed one of us down here there wasn't a damned thing we could do about it. It could not even be reported. So these men were putting up a good fight, and there wasn't just six of them like on the other patrols. There were a dozen men with this herd. Twice the number than we had encountered in the past. It was as though they knew our force beforehand and the night we would go out.

Our movements were always subject to spies that we knew existed in cities like El Paso. Even the Comanche had spies as did a number of outlaw gangs and stagecoach robbers. Without inside information, they would never know which stages were loaded with gold or silver and when the Marshal or Texas Rangers were otherwise occupied.

But this kind of informant probably came from our very own Ranger Post. I never told anyone but the Sergeants when we are going to ride into Mexico illegally. The men find out at supper, maybe three or four hours before we ride out. Then again, I have never had a Texas Ranger break bad on me either. So it was something that I did have a hard time believing. I suppose it could have just been blind luck and coincidence, but then again, I have never been a big believer in coincidence. Although Rowdy Bates had got me to believe a bit in luck.

As the dozen Mexican rustlers came towards us, the hair on the back of my neck stood on end, and goose-bumps covered my arms. I pulled my two .44 Colt Pattersons and set the spurs to Horse, and he leaped into action. At the same time, Weston and Bees came riding closing in on the outlaws from both flanks. There was gunfire coming and going now. I began to shoot off my right revolver and then my left as my horse ran flat out. Flame and gun smoke came from the barrels of some two dozen guns. But in the crossfire, the outlaws didn't have a chance. We killed them to the last man, and only one of my men was wounded. Billy Joe was shot in the ear. The bullet blew his earlobe clean off, but the top part of his ear was intact.

We pulled up to check on the men and collect their weapons and any money or gold they might have on them then I mounted Horse.

"Ain't we going to dig their graves, boss?" Toby Bees asked.

"You stop to dig one grave you best dig one for yourself, son. I feel it won't be long until someone comes along. There were too many men in that bunch of rustlers. I figure we best ride north and on out of here right now. Whoever is coming can bury the dead. It is most likely their men who perished at any rate."

We drove the cattle north at double the pace we usually do. Now knowing that we have finally gotten the attention of old Pedro Mendez. And he intends to stop us if he can. When we crossed the river, the men began to slow down with their horses.

"Keep pushing for a few miles more men," I ordered as I moved north again. "If we can go into Mexico to catch rustlers I reckon Mendez can send men north of the border to catch us. But they won't stray too far into Texan territory. Just like we don't venture too far south. Always keeping in mind an escape if necessary.

We pushed the cattle and a few loose horses all the way to Windy Ridge Ranch. I figure that not even Mendez would be so brash as to rustle cattle from the ranch of a bunch of Texas Rangers. So we pushed on until I saw the ranch house down there in the little valley.

Standing on the porch with her hands bunched up into fists and perched on her hips Lola Zapata inspected us as we rode in. The Rangers moved the cattle to our ever growing corals, and I rode right over to where Lola and Bill Vents stood.

"It looks like you had a good run, Captain," Bill observed. "But I don't see any rustlers."

"This bunch put up a bit of a fight, but we got them in a crossfire, Bill. Howdy Honey Bunch," I said to Lola as I gave her a long hug.

"What's the matter Ridge?" Lola asked as she clung to me.

"I don't rightly know. I guess it's just that things are working out too well these days," I said as I pondered on my feelings. "It would appear that I have been bestowed with a whirlwind of influences of late."

"That is hardly something to worry about, Honey. You men are always worrying about something. It's like a law of nature. Nothing is going to happen."

CHAPTER 16:

LONE STAR SALOON

"I can't believe that we are back at home after such a long mission," Travis Picket said.

"I can't believe that we're here without the Captain, Sergeants Vents and Smith and my old pal Toby Bees," Captain Rowdy Bates replied. "I reckon I miss the old gang."

"Ain't I part of the old gang?" Travis asked, somewhat offended.

"Sure you are, but it was different with the Captain. You know what I mean. It just ain't the same."

"Things always change, and it never is the same," Travis replied. "So why should this be any different. We have to deal with whatever life throws at us, Captain Bates. If it weren't for change, you wouldn't be in charge of the Laredo Texas Ranger Post."

"You're right about that Pard. But we still have to see if it was a blessing or a curse. Oh, I wanted to be Captain alright. But now that I'm here and all it just seems that I bit off much more than I can chew."

"Don't worry about you biting off more than you can chew, Rowdy," Travis chuckled. "Your mouth is probably a whole lot bigger than you think."

Justin Burrs came over to the table that the two Rangers occupied and asked, "How about a couple more shots of whiskey, Captain?"

"We best drink coffee for a spell, Justin," Rowdy replied. "It's early in the day. Y'all still have the town hearings here?"

"Part of the time. Since Judge Roy Bean bought a plot of land down by Rick Pawless, he passes half his time holding court in his own saloon that he built right there beside the trading post and the other half here. But we ain't had a good hanging for quite a spell now."

"Other than the lack of hangings has there been anything going on in Laredo that I should know about?" Rowdy asked the saloon owner.

"If you want to know what's been going on in town there comes Sheriff Deeds right now," Justin said.

"Damn, normally Deeds don't give us nothing but bad news or something he don't fancy tending to," the new Laredo Captain replied.

"Howdy Marshal," Toby and Travis said at the same time.

"Morning Ranger Picket and Sergeant Bates."

"It ain't Sergeant Bates anymore, Marshal, nor is it Ranger Picket," Travis informed the town lawman.

"Did something happen to Captain Creek?" Deeds asked.

"No, nothing's happened to Ridge," Rowdy replied. "He's just been transferred to El Paso to deal with the rustlers and the problems on the border."

"Rowdy was made Captain and me Sergeant to take over the men here in town," Travis continued.

"Well, I'll be a son of a gun," Marshal Deeds stated. "But Ridge has been Captain here in Laredo since John RIP Ford left before the Civil War. It ain't going to be the same around here with Captain Creek gone."

"Don't worry none, Marshal," Rowdy assured the local lawman. "Ridge wouldn't have promoted me to Captain and sent me back here if I weren't up to the task."

"It's just that I don't like it when things change, me being a creature of habit and all," the

Marshal replied. "Actually the last trouble we had in town was when that old Scotsman rode through with that mess of European folks on his wagon train. There were so many people in that bunch that they damned near filled the town up. They left trash lay about all over the place. Never seen such a bunch of folks throw so many goods away. Lucky for us they stayed just on the edge of town and not here in the center. But they still caused more ruckus than I would have preferred."

"That lot won't be creating any more ruckus, Deeds," the new Captain replied. "They're all six feet under. They tried to go up against the Captain, and he and the Comanche finished the bunch of them off. Except for a few stragglers that we found that had escaped the war party. But the Comanche had done killed the old man Lord Bogardus. So he won't be coming back."

"That don't surprise me none," Deeds replied. "They didn't seem to have much notion as to how to travel out in the wild country. I had heard that they had up to some fifty Comanche following them just for the spoils that they left behind. I figured it was just a matter of time before the Braves got tired of picking up after them and went at them head-on."

"Where did you get that much information?" the Captain asked.

"Why from Fannie Porter," he replied. "She went over to San Antonio to tend to one of her other saloons, Tilly Howards when she ran into the old cuss. She said he shot and killed that famous Russian nobleman in a duel of all things. She's back here in the Gentlemen's Club again. She has taken a fancy to Laredo and stays here more than in the big city nowadays. That with an occasional visit up north to Kansas where she opened two more saloons. With the big cattle drives that head to Abilene there are more customers for the taverns and dance halls than ever. Fannie must be so rich now that she probably don't even know how much money she makes a month."

"If Fannie is in town I figure we best go over and see her," Rowdy Bates said with a childish grin. "Just wait until I tell her I'm a Texas Ranger Captain now. I bet that will surprise her."

After a while, Frances Cooks, Virgil Hatch, Buck Hacket, and Gus Gavin along with a few more of the boys arrived at the Lone Star Saloon. The Rangers pushed three tables together with chairs for each man placed around the circle of seats. Each and every one of them still curious as to the latest events and changes in the local Texas Rangers, although they had been briefed by Sergeant Picket.

"How is it that Austin made such a radical change in things for us here in Laredo?" Frances, the Ranger Post cook asked.

"I reckon you'll have to ask the Majors that, Cooks," Captain Bates replied. "We just follow orders. Ridge was told to reform the old El Paso post and to pick a Captain for Laredo. The why and what of our superior officer's orders ain't any business of mine. I just act on them as I get them, Frances."

"The easiest way to eat crow is while it is still warm," Travis added. "The colder it gets, the harder it is to swallow. So we best just move on and get to it."

"You mean Captain Creek really ain't coming back to Laredo?" Butch Emmitt asked. "Ever?"

"That you know as much about as I do," Bates confirmed. "Ridge got orders from Austin with no detailed explanation, and he duly acted on them as he was expected to do by his superiors. He gave me an order to come here and take charge, which actually surprised me even though I have always wanted to be a captain. But I don't go questioning my boss as to the why and what of things. I just do as ordered, as I expect you men to do as well. If Captain Creek sent me here, it's because he reckons I can do the job so I would appreciate it if all you boys worked with me."

"Why wasn't I made Sergeant as I am already a Corporal?" Frances Cooks asked.

"Then who would do the cooking Frances?" Rowdy answered. "Ridge kept Humphrey Willow on with him because he makes pies, baked apples and all to fancy the Captain's sweet tooth, so you're the only cook we have. If you were a sergeant, you wouldn't have time to be our cook. Do any of you other men know how to do more than boil an egg? That's what I thought. I made Travis our Sergeant as he is a good leader and has more experience than most of you men. But he too has to prove himself just like I do. So I would appreciate if all you men cooperate the best you can. Time will tell if Travis and I are cut out for the jobs."

"I hear they got some new ladies over at the Gentlemen's club," Caleb Hatch informed his buddies. "Why don't we go on over and have a peek? It don't cost nothing to look."

"That's what I was just saying to Travis," Rowdy agreed. "Let's go have some fun. The day after tomorrow we will be riding out to get you boy's back in shape. You all been sitting around Laredo for too long. We got to be sharp if we are to head out into the wild country. There's plenty of Comanche and outlaws about."

CHAPTER 17:

FANCY MEXICAN SADDLE

Pedro Mendez was sitting on his ranch house porch at a table reading the weekly newspaper. Just a few hours south of the Rio Grande and the border with Mexico when Texas Ranger Corporal Festus Willis came riding up as agreed.

"Howdy, Señor Mendez," he said to the infamous ranch baron. "Here I am just as you ordered. I'm on a four day leave, so I ain't in a big hurry to get back to the El Paso."

"Step down off of your horse and take a seat," Mendez said without taking his eyes off of his newspaper. "How is Captain Creek taking to you Willis?"

"At the moment he ain't taking to me all that well, I reckon," Willis replied. "So far, he has not accepted the new Ranger recruits or me into his fold, so my information is limited. But I have ears, and his other men talk loads when they have a belly full of whiskey."

"It's your job to make Creek trust you, damn it. I pay you far too much for no more information than that!"

"I did find out that on their last raid south of the border they met with considerable resistance. So the information that I have given you so far may have been scarce but factual. I figure you are going to have to go some to stop Creek. He is about as hard a man as I've ever met, Señor."

"I don't swim in that shit! So what do you have new for me now?" Mendez asked as he folded up his newspaper and put it down on the table.

"Creek has a ranch a-ways north of the border that he's stocking up with the cattle he confiscates from your rustlers," Willis went on. "Since nobody knows who the livestock belongs to nobody is complaining about him building up his own ranch with cattle he takes from Mexico. In Texas, there ain't no law against stealing Mexican cattle and bringing them back across the border."

"When is he planning to go out again and how many men does he take with him on patrol?" Mendez asked. "I'll also need to know exactly where he plans to cross into Mexico on his next raid. I intend to put a stop to this business of him stealing all my rustled cattle. And what do you find so funny Mister Willis?"

"I was just pondering on the fact that the same cattle may well have been rustled three or four times already. It seems that cattle are being stolen from one side of the border or the other pretty much every night," Festus replied. "I intended nothing by it. It just seems odd that no one has any idea of who these cattle really belong to."

"I know who those damned cattle belong to!" Mendez refuted as he slammed his hand down on the table before him. "They belong to me! As will the land north of the Rio Grande once I get this Ranger business sorted out. And not to the Texans! Colonel Colt made all men equal and I intend to prove it."

"Whatever you say, boss," Willis said as he stifled a chuckle.

"Did you find out where Captain Creek's kin folk live?"

"That was easy," Festus replied. "He told me that much himself even though he ain't exactly a man on the talkative side. It's a place called Ragged Ridge Creek. Sounds like some little shithole mostly populated by poor folks. It's a few days ride northwest of Laredo."

"Family is family, whether they are poor or rich. You can stay here tonight and rest, then turn your ass around and head back to El Paso tomorrow morning," Mendez ordered. "You'll find grub in the chow hall. I'll be planning a welcome party for Creek and his Rangers on his next raiding patrol south. And he won't be coming back if I have anything to say about it."

With that Pedro Mendez stood to his feet and walked over to the hitching post and his horse. He unwrapped his reins from the rail and lifted his left boot into the stirrup of the fancy Mexican saddle full of silver studs that sparkled in the sunlight. Grabbing his saddle horn and cantle as he pulled himself astride his mount. He turned the animal without another word and put his fancy silver spurs to his horse's flanks and rode off. Leaving Festus Willis to stew at the lack of respect he had bestowed on the Corporal.

But at least Mendez paid Willis well, which was something more than he could say about the measly salary he received from the Texas Rangers. As soon as Creek was dead, Festus planned to come back down here and ask Mendez for a job on his ranch. After his information proves to be reliable, the Mexican rancher should trust the Corporal more. Festus was now looking forward to a future life of luxury, at least when compared to the life he led now. Living in the Ranger bunkhouse with fourteen snoring veterans and recruits. It was enough to drive a sane man crazy.

But the Mendez Ranch was a place of luxury when compared to the Ranger post in El Paso. The main house was a large U-shaped building with five bedrooms, two living rooms, Señor Mendez's office, and library along with a huge kitchen where the ranch baron's meals were prepared along with the ranch hands and gun hands alike. Here Señor Mendez and his closest men lived a life of luxury compared to El Paso.

Sure the nightlife in El Paso on the Texan side of the border was wild and entertaining, but Paso del Norte on the Mexican side was bigger and had as many saloons and dance halls as on the north side. But there were a lot fewer Texans, which didn't disappoint Festus none. He got on well with the men from south of the border even if a lot of them were ornery types. No, there ain't a yellow bone in these boys' bodies. All of the men who worked regular like for Mendez had proved their skills and loyalty. Something that Festus hoped his last bit of information would change the boss's assessment of his new spy and treat him like his most loyal men.

Festus headed on over to the chow hall, and he was promptly served with a beef stew and freshly baked biscuits. The stew was heaping with chunks of tender beef, potatoes, peas, onions, and carrots. Mighty tasty. And there was some kind of pudding for dessert.

The other men that worked for Mendez were even nice to Festus. There seemed to be a certain amount of comradeship among the hired hands at the Mendez Ranch. Treating Festus as an equal already. Something that the boss had yet to do. Then again bosses were often aloof with their hired men so as to not get too close for when they had to give hard orders in a violent situation.

Yeah, Festus reckoned things would be right fine living down here in Mexico as soon as Pedro Mendez kills Captain Creek. That uppity Texas Ranger had never treated Festus Willis with much more than contempt and suspicion. And he had no cause, at least no reason that Creek should be aware of, thought the spy as he chuckled. He reckoned that he would indeed get the last laugh when that lawman was dying, bleeding out in the dust as he deserved.

CHAPTER 18:

ON THE RUN

We rode out of El Paso just as the sun's fiery ball neared the edge of the world. Tossing light across the sky in a variety of reds, oranges, and yellows. As usual, we would ride out the north end of town and keep riding a-ways until we turned east to swing wide of the city. Just in the case, somebody was following that Tuc and Potak didn't see. Then when the two Tonkawa rode up and gave us the all clear we turned south towards Mexico and whatever it is that awaits us. Today being like any other day when the Tonkawa told us nobody was following us we headed for the Rio Grande. On the last trip, they expected us as there were twice as many men that rode with the cattle as the other times. Quickly locating our patrol due it's the size.

So today we moved towards another spot in the river to cross into Mexico with fewer men than the last patrol. With there just being six of us tonight it would be easier to hide with less than a half moon to lead the way. Moving from one shadow to another just like Potak had taught us to. Especially if we split up into two groups of three. As we arrived at the river, I told Tuc and Potak to head back to El Paso and that we would be along shortly.

I hated to doubt the loyalty of any of our men but someone is passing on information about our patrols, and those two Tonkawa are the worst gossips I have ever known. Best to be careful now until I can figure out who our rat is. I rode over the river with Weston, Toby, Humphrey, Ace and Billy Joe. Leaving Clinton Westwood back at the post to keep an eye on the rest of the men. Looking out for anybody acting suspiciously. I selected only men I trusted one-hundred percent. I left Bill Vents back at the ranch with the three ranch hands and sent Lola packing back to El Paso.

Until I found out who is talking, I planned to button everything up as tight as possible. Suspecting everybody but my closest Rangers. Even though I hate to say it, the culprit could even be Lola herself. I ain't known her long, and she is from the other side of the border. A thing that I doubt but at this point, I don't plan to take any chances until I get this last herd of cattle. And then I plan to find Mendez and hang him. Be it here south of the border or not. This is going to end shortly. And the only way to do it is with the death of the Mexican ranch baron.

"You really think we got a spy inside the Ranger Post?" Weston Smith asked me.

"I can't prove it, but since thinking don't cost nothing, I can think it, and I do," I replied.

When we got a ways past the Rio Grande, we split up into two groups. Weston took Ace and Billy Joe, and Toby and Humphrey went with me. We agreed that after an hour of one bunch heading east and the other heading west, each group would ride south to seek out rustlers. After we rode south two hours, we would turn towards each other until we made contact again and then if we had no results we would repeat the procedure once more before riding north for Texas. I had no plans to be in Mexico during the day. Then there could be soldiers from the Mexican Army riding the border hunting for lawmen and rustlers just like us.

I rode out front with Toby Bees following while Humphrey took up the rear with his eight-gage scatter-gun sitting in the crook of his stump of an arm. We moved south without mishap for two hours then we turned west to meet back up with our other patrol.

After a good spell riding Toby Bees said, "I figure we should run into Weston and the boys any minute now, boss."

I looked up at the moon to judge our time and replied, "I reckon you're right, son. We best slow down a mite so we can hear any noises. I don't want Weston shooting at us."

"I bet Weston don't want Humphrey shooting at him with that big old cannon either," Toby giggled, making him seem even younger than he was.

"You don't have that thing cocked, do you, Ranger Willow?" I asked.

"As a matter of fact I do, Captain. But don't worry, I won't shoot Weston although I have had a mind to at times," Ranger Willow said with a chuckle.

Just then we heard gunfire from nearby. Maybe a half-dozen shots or so.

———

What even the Mendez men that sat waiting for the Texas Rangers to pass didn't know was that Pedro, their boss, had already sent another dozen men to Ragged Ridge Creek, Texas to kill everybody in that little shithole of a town. Especially the family of Ranger Creek. He had told them to spread the word that the famous Ranger himself had done the killing. They were to burn the little town to the ground and report it to the nearest Marshal's office. Then when they found him dead in Mexico, nobody would care or come looking for another lawman that broke-bad. And nobody would be the wiser that Mendez was behind the whole thing. He would finally be rid of Creek and his Rangers. Free to carry on with his designs on the cattle and land north of the Mexican border.

Pedro Mendez had hidden with his men in a blind right by the trail he had expected Creek's men to ride down. The Mexican rancher had five-man patrols spread all across the border area. All of the men taking every precaution to move with stealth so as not to end up on the shooting end of Captain Creek's Colts. Along with Mendez, he had three of his best men and his thirteen-year-old nephew, Armando. He was a nephew on his wife's side. Another worthless relative that his wife had brought to the ranch expecting for him to hand them some land and cattle so they can all start up their own spreads.

Something that Señor Mendez had no intention of doing. But to keep his wife from nagging on him, he decided to bring the little shit-for-brains along with him tonight. The boy just might work out for killing folks as even though he was young, he seemed to have a lust for blood. When he told the boy, they were headed out to bushwhack a few Texans he jumped at the chance to be part of the bloodletting.

Mendez's nephew, Armando had a considerable mean streak in him. He enjoyed torturing helpless animals and was eager to shoot and kill his first Texan. The boy was young in years, but he had already turned evil and was up for any violence that would present itself. He wore two .45 Colt revolvers, and he knew how to use them. He reckoned he was about as fast as any of the men that worked for his uncle. Having the confidence that young men often possessed even without ever testing their grit or skills on other men with weapons. Especially men who live and die by the gun like those stinking Texas Rangers.

Armando had run into some of the US Army boys when riding with his uncle north of the border on cattle business. Of the soldiers, he had observed in the forts that are scattered across the state he had mostly seen men too drunk and bored to make much resistance. Especially when facing first rate gun-hands from Mexico.

Now he sat with his uncle and three other gunslingers from the Mendes ranch. Each of the men carried several weapons such as rifles, pistols and large knives. Each and every one, calm and relaxed even though they know they were hunting one dangerous hombre.

So the five men took cover behind some rocks and quietly sat and waited until one of the Texan lawmen showed themselves. Then they planned to bushwhack them or even capture one or two of them to hang back at the Mendez ranch. Armando was of course wishing and hoping it would be Captain Creek they would catch and hang. The young mean teenage Mexican had yet to see his first hanging, and he wanted to be part of it.

They sat there hiding behind the rocks for two hours before they heard the first sound from one of the Texas Ranger's horses as they approached. In short order one Ranger sergeant and two of his men rode in single file, carefully moving forward oblivious of the men waiting nearby to bushwhack them.

As soon as the three men came into view, the five Mexicans opened fire from the rocks with their Winchesters. The two Rangers behind the sergeant went down with the first volley as did their horses. The sergeant's horse was shot and killed as well, but as he fell from his dying mount, he rolled and came up running towards the Mexicans with both guns blazing. One of his bullet hit Mendez's oldest gun hand, shot right between the eyes. But the other four Mexicans gunned him down in his tracks. Weston Smith was hit by three bullets to the chest killing him dead before he hit the dirt.

———

As soon as I heard the gunfire the hair on the back of my neck stood on end, and goosebumps covered my arms, and I went into a red rage. I immediately spurred Horse forward toward the sound of the gunshots and Humphrey, and Toby Bees followed. Each man with his weapons in hand ready to come to the rescue of our fellow Rangers.

Visibility was not as good as I would have liked, even with the little amount of moonlight. As I neared the point of conflict, I could see three dead horses and three men on the trail in front of me.

The gunfire started immediately from a crop of rocks to my right. I swung both my guns toward the powder flashes and began to fire wherever I saw a flame from a gun-barrel. Humphrey came up fast on my right with the scatter-gun leveled at the rocks and let both barrels loose just as he was shot in the face. The impact of the Winchester rifle round knocked him right off the back of his horse and to the ground in a big puff of dust.

I looked to my left and saw Toby Bees riding by fast, hanging down low from the side of his saddle, firing his revolver as his arm lay across the back of his horse. His horse received a bullet to the head and fell directly on top of Toby. I could hear the snap of his neck even amidst the gunfire. Now I was in as deep a red rage as I had ever been in. All caution now seemed pointless. Five of my closest men lay dead or dying in the dirt beside me.

I slid from my saddle to the ground to give the attackers less target to shoot at and walked towards the gunfire at a furious pace. Pouring led into the gunmen hiding behind the rocks. As two men rose with rifles poised to shoot me, I pulled both triggers and killed them both before they got a shot off. Now I saw that only two men remained. Both Mexicans were now shaken up some as I came at them in all my fury. Then I saw that the old Mexican was Pedro Mendez himself so I dropped my .44s to the ground and pulled my 45's and put a bullet into each lung of the old Mexican bandit.

The last man standing seemed to be on the small side and was now frozen with fright. But he was no innocent bystander as I had seen him shoot Toby Bees' horse. The man aimed his rifle at me as I looked deep into his frightened eyes. His shot went wide, and I put a half dozen bullets into the man's body as I took revenge on them murdering my men.

As the silence came from the lack of gunfire, my red rage went on. I stomped over to the five dead Mexicans and kicked and shot each man a number of times more. Now not knowing what I was doing other than seeking revenge on anything I could.

As I noted that my pistol's hammers were landing on empty chambers, I stopped pulling the triggers. I looked over at Humphrey and Weston, and I could clearly see that they were both dead. I then carefully walked over to where Toby Bees lay. His eyes were wide open with fright as his broken neck seemed to twitch about all on its own. Toby mouthed some words, and even though no sound came out, I could read his lips. He was asking me if he was dead.

I dropped to the ground and knelt beside the boy I had taken to as if he were my own son. Keeping watch over him the best that I could. But it just wasn't enough. I should have known better to bring him along with me on such a mission. And Weston here was my best friend. We had worked together for the last twenty years.

I lay my hands on Toby's chest and said, "Now don't you worry son. I'm not going to let you die on me."

But the boy's head made one last jerk and the Sergeant's eyes went blank. I laid his head in my lap and sat there for I don't know how long. I could feel streams of salty water run down my cheeks as I held the brave young Ranger in my arms. As daylight broke, I finally got to my feet and went back to where Mendez lay. Right where I had shot him. I pulled off his boots and removed his spurs. Then I walked back to where they had hidden their horses and led them to where my men lay dead. I took each of the five men and put them over the backs of the Mexican's horses and tied them tight. Then I removed the old Pedro Mendez's saddle and put it on Horse. I mounted up and took the reins of the five animals and led them towards the border and Texas.

I felt the least I could do is take them back to Texas and to our ranch to bury. So they could rest in peace at their new home. I knew there would be other Mexican men looking for me as I headed for the border, so I kept my weapons at the ready. But as luck would have it, I made it to the river without being discovered. And I didn't stop riding until I saw the small ranch house there in the valley. Another tear ran down the side of my face, and I consciously wiped it away with the sleeve of my shirt.

As I neared the ranch house, my old mentor, Bill Vents came out the door and stepped onto the porch. He held his hand over his eyes to block the sun to see better who was coming. As soon as the old man saw me leading the five burdened horses, he sat down hard on the chair behind him. Then he buried his face in his hands, and I could see his shoulders shake and shudder as the man wept for our loss.

That afternoon I dug a hole for each of my five friends just a ways from the ranch house. Bill was too distraught even to lift a shovel. Just sitting there on the porch chair staring off into space. I reckon he was trying to figure out why such a thing would happen. Even though he knew that whenever we ventured into the wild country, anything could and does happen. But I felt he took the death of Toby Bees especially hard. He just sat there with Stinky the dog in his arms as he rocked back and forth. Nearly in a state of shock of what had transpired.

I sat by the buried men the entire day as did the hard old Texas Ranger Sergeant. I had made each man a wooden cross and Bill had carved their names on each one.

"You know they are going to be coming after you, don't you Ridge," Bill Vents finally said. "Pedro Mendez was Mexican but also claimed Texan residence. Him being such an important man in the Cattlemen's Association and all it will demand that they put a bounty on your head. You'll be a wanted man now, Captain. You best pack your traveling kit and ride hell for leather on out of these parts until we can prove you aren't guilty of murdering Mendez. I'll tend to Horse for you and get you two extra mounts ready while you collect whatever you want to take with you."

It slowly started to sink in what had happened. I myself had unknowingly crossed that blurry grey line between the legal and the illegal. Now I find myself a wanted man. Much like many of the ex-lawmen that I have chased down and hung over the years as a Texas Ranger.

I walked into the ranch house and pulled out my two .44 Pattersons and my two Peacemakers and dismantled each, one at a time, making sure my weapons were clean and in good working order. I even took the little derringer that I had taken off of Maggie Murdock from Westchester, Ohio after she killed that city dandy who was abusing her. It just might come in handy with me on the run and all. I put the two Peacemakers in my saddlebags along with a leather pouch of gold dust that I had saved up and my coffee and small campfire kettle. That and a long coat and some cheroots with bright green strings tied around them.

When I was done, I found Bill Vents sitting out on the porch with the horses all ready, waiting on me.

"What's the Mexican saddle for Ridge?" the Sergeant asked. "It ain't yours."

"I mean for it to be a calling card for any men that are sent after me for killing Mendez. Kind of letting them know it's me and I'm waiting for them. I may have to run now, but I don't plan on letting this go until all of the Mendez's men are dead and his ranch is burned to the ground."

"But the man is already kilt, Ridge," Bill replied. "You can't do no more to hurt him."

"I can see to it that his family joins him in Hell," I said as I took my longtime friend's hand and squeezed it in my own.

"Sometimes things fall apart to make way for better times, Ridge," old Bill Vents said with a tear in his eye. "Every trail has its puddles."

"When a man goes out he goes out broke," I replied in a choked up voice. "Everything in life is on loan anyway. I intend to seek restitution even if it costs me my own life."

Saying goodbye to my oldest friend alive, Texas Ranger Sergeant Bill Vents. In his hand, I left a signed paper passing my ranch over to the hard old storyteller. At least now Bill can settle down as I dreamed of doing. But I can now see that my path has taken a bad course and settling down was not in the cards for me. I should have known it was too good to be true.

"Tell Lola it just weren't meant to be," I instructed my old mentor.

I turned to Horse, mounted up and rode off without even glancing back. Knowing that soon every lawman and bounty hunter in southwestern Texas will be on my trail. There will no doubt be a bounty on my head for killing Mendez. Money is more important than most things, so I reckon nobody will be interested in hearing my side of the story. They will be more intent on killing me and claiming the bounty money.

I rode north for seven days, putting as much ground between me and Windy Ridge

Ranch as possible. Keeping my eyes peeled for gunslingers following my trail. It was at the end of the seventh day when the light was just starting to dim on the horizon that I saw the first cloud of dust behind me. I pulled Horse up for a moment and calculated that considering the size of the dust cloud it must be two or three men.

I turned Horse and dug in the new silver Mexican spurs and rode north at a quick gallop. Hoping to find a spot to hide in wait and use my Sharps rifle to thin out my opponents. But as luck would have it, I was riding through some flatlands, and there was no cover anywhere. And with Horse now running tired from the long day they were gaining on me. I turned in my saddle and now could clearly see two men riding hell bent for leather intent on catching up with me.

I pushed Horse for all his was worth as the two men were now in Winchester rifle range. I heard a few cracks of rifle fire and suddenly felt something like a sledgehammer hit me in the head. A bullet had made a deep graze alongside my skull. But although dizzy and nearly faint I spurred Horse on into the closing night and to safety from the hunters on my trail. As I rode Hollis-Bolus into the dark, I felt myself become dizzier, and I watched in my mind's eye as I fell off of Horse. Hitting the ground hard and losing all sense of direction and eventually consciousness.

CHAPTER 19:

BUSHWHACKED

It was midday, and the sun in this part of Texas was blistering hot. The two black vultures were just standing yards away, maybe about twenty feet from the body which lay there in the dirt. A stream of blood ran slowly from the man's head into the fine dust. As it made a puddle in the sand, it dried out and hardened as quickly as it appeared.

The vultures seemed not to be sure if the animal was dead or alive. Not entirely confident enough that the meal before them was harmless. It was some animal instinct that told them not to trust this creature as he still may be very dangerous.

I didn't know why it was so dark and what were those bright red dots in the middle of my eyes? It took me a few minutes to realize that it is I, and I am not dead, at least not yet. My head felt like a piece of heavy steel, far too heavy to pick up and support itself on my shoulders. I tried to move, but I couldn't even get my eyes to open.

Something seemed to have dried over my eyes, and they were stuck together. Little by little I started to come around, and I lifted my hand up to pry them open. Once I opened my eyes, I could see that my hands were covered in my own blood. That must be why my head hurts so, but I'll be damned if I can remember a thing. Not even who I am or how I got here.

I propped myself up on one elbow and had a look to try to see where I was. Or if in fact, this was Hell but all I saw was hot Texas desert. There was a horse nearby. Could that be my horse? Now when I looked down, I saw that I was armed with two worn .44 Colt Patterson revolvers. Who am I and how did I get here? As I pushed myself into a sitting position, I shaded my eyes with my hand and had a good look around me. Other than prairie bushes and dirt there was not a thing visible, apart from the two vultures standing by to see if I would allow them dinner, although that was not in my plans.

I didn't know what to think. I have no memory of my name, where I live or what I do. I had a look at the backs of my hands, and they were rough and scarred. My right wrist seemed to have a scar from a bullet hole on it. I struggled to my feet and slowly limped to the black and beige stallion.

I didn't want to scare him, but there seemed no need to move carefully as the horse clearly knew who I was, if only I could ask the animal. Maybe I'll find a clue of something in the saddlebags strapped across his back, just behind the fancy Mexican saddle.

I untied and pulled the saddlebags from off the horse and knelt down, having a look at what I had. When I removed the leather tie attached to the flap on the saddle bag it opened with ease.

But on this side, there was only a bit of dried beef, a coffee kettle, some biscuits, cheroots, and a long coat. When I pulled the leather tie on the other side, I was surprised at what I found. There were two more worn Colt .45 Peacekeeper revolvers, a small two-shot derringer, a Bowie knife and lots of rounds for .44s, .45s and .50-120 rifle shells. There was also a small leather bag of gold dust. I had no idea what I needed with so many weapons, but at least I ain't broke.

There was a sheath on this side of the saddle with a Winchester Repeater in it. On the other side, in another scabbard, there was a Sharps rifle with a long brass scope like they used to hunt buffalo. The brass scope was as long as the barrel, a big heavy gun for long range shooting. The stocks were worn and shiny with use, the wood dark from oil. The Mexican saddle was sparkling from all the metal studs with which it was decorated. Was I Mexican? No, I'd be thinking in Mexican if I were from south of the border.

I pulled the canteen from the saddle horn and had a good drink of hot water, sensing that I should not drink too much. Not knowing where I am didn't help in giving me a direction to go in. Out beyond the two vultures, it seemed like nothing but sand and dirt. Looking in the other direction, I think I can just make out some hills in the hazy distance. I struggled onto the horse with the fancy saddle and turned it towards the blurry hill-like outline.

I rode all through the day for some six or seven hours till the sun finally relinquished some of its draining power and then on into the night. Sometime during the night, I must have fallen off my horse as when the morning sun started to burn into my skin I came to again. My horse was standing just a few yards from my body. When my head cleared, I slowly rose to my feet and once again I mounted up and rode on into the hills.

In the distance, I think I can hear some running water, so I headed in the direction of the noise. After a short ride, I came to a small spring that ran out of a flat rock on the side of the hill and formed a small water hole. I cautiously neared the water, and I could see that there were no hoof-prints, so no one on horseback had been here recently. When I arrived at the waterhole, my horse seemed calm, so while still mounted I had a look around me as my horse refreshed himself. When I felt sure that there was no danger, I climbed down off of my mount and dropped to my knees at the water's edge. I first cleaned my hands then I splashed water on my face and the bullet crease in the side of my head. Then, I washed off the blood and dirt and had my first look at the water's reflection of my own face. I was shocked at what I saw.

Leaning forward looking at the reflection in the water was a hard face. A scar ran across the forehead and another long scar from one ear to my chin.   A rugged, yet handsome face. The frightening thing were those eyes in the reflection of the pool of water. They were the color of gray steel, hard and cold as though they were a dead man's eyes. Not what I expected to see in my own reflection. Who was I? Or better yet, what am I?

As I mounted my horse, I moved off again into the same direction I had ridden all day and all last night. In the distance, I saw the outline of a small town. From this far it didn't appear to be much more than two rows of clapboard buildings and tent stores on one main street. As I neared, I passed a sign stating the town's name. It was called "Infierno."

I'm not Mexican, but I know what Infierno is. It was the word for Hell in Spanish. The thought crossed my mind that maybe I am dead after all. I didn't feel dead, but I didn't feel alive either. Ever since I had seen my eyes in that water hole, I'm not sure what I am. Since then I have become aware that I don't sense fear of any kind, only the nagging curiosity from the darkness of having no memory of my past.

When I rode into town, it was just waking up. A few horses were standing around tied up by the saloon and one in front of what I would guess to be the marshal's office. Other than a couple of chickens and a rooster, it was just two rows of dilapidated buildings and a dusty street if you want to call it that.

I rode on over to the saloon and dismounted, wrapping the reins of the horse around the hitching rail. In front, there were a couple of empty chairs on the porch on either side of the saloon's bat-wing doors. When my boots landed on the boardwalk in front of the saloon, I just became aware of the noise from my spurs. It was a sound that I was so used to that I didn't notice its presence. I looked down and saw I wore fancy silver Mexican spurs on my worn leather boots.

The wood on the boardwalk groaned with every step, along with the jingling noise of my star-shaped spurs. I approached the entrance to the saloon, and I stopped to have a look around behind me to make sure nobody was following. Then I peered inside the dark room over the swinging doors. There seemed to be about a dozen patrons imbibing within. Some drinking coffee and others, apparently having spent the night were still drunk. A sleepy looking bartender stood at the bar with his head propped up by one arm with his elbow resting on the bar-top.

Nobody in the saloon seemed to present a threat, so I pushed the two swinging doors inward and took two steps forward. I stopped for a couple of seconds so my eyes could adjust to the dark saloon. Now I took the seven paces to the bar and ordered a whiskey. The bartender didn't seem very interested in his new customer.

"Hey, barkeep! Give me a whiskey, please," I repeated myself.

When the man continued to ignore me, I pulled out one of my .44's and smacked him across the face with it. I apparently don't tolerate bad manners in a man, although my actions surprised even me. It was as though I was conditioned and had no will of my own. I took a couple of steps to behind the bar and pulled a bottle of whiskey from the shelf and a shot glass. Then I slowly moved to the table in the corner and sat in the chair with my back to the walls, all the time carefully observing every person in the saloon. One man looked over at me as though he was going to make some comment, but when we made eye contact, he looked down at the table in front of him and kept his words to himself. I felt the same way when I saw my cold dead eyes in the water-hole reflection that very morning.

I drank the shot of whiskey a sip at a time being aware of the burning sensation in my desert-dry throat. I heard the barkeeper start moving behind the bar where he had fallen after being slugged by my .44's barrel. Now when he stood up and looked deeply into my cold dead eyes, I saw the fear on his face.

"Sorry Mister," he said. "In the mornings my manners ain't what they should be." He hurried over and poured me another shot of whiskey saying, "Those whiskeys are on the house. Forgive my bad manners, Mister."

I just looked at him and let him pour me another drink.

"I don't tolerate bad manners in a man or a woman for that matter," I casually replied.

He hurried back to behind the bar where he started busying himself with polishing up the glassware on the shelf, trying his best to cover up his fear.

After slowly sipping my second shot of whiskey I called out to the barkeep. "Bring me a pot of coffee and a cup and take this bottle of whiskey with you."

I somehow knew I shouldn't drink so much as to make me lose my edge. Why? I still don't know. It was hot in the saloon even though it was still early. The hot Texas sun was not yet up far enough in the sky to provide the intense heat it will soon bring.

While I was sitting there minding my coffee a man walked up to the saloon doors. Then I could see the dirty boots of a second man stepping up behind him. They too were checking out what was in the dark saloon before entering, but I doubt they saw me back here in the corner. As the first gunslinger pushed his way into the tavern, I saw a rugged unshaven man. He was covered in the same dust I was and was carrying a Colt .45 slung low on his leg and tied down to his thigh. He and his partner, also packing a side-arm, walked up to the now very awake barkeep.

"Give us a couple of whiskeys," said the first man to the bartender.

While the whiskeys were poured, the first stranger spent his time scanning the room through the big mirror behind the saloon bar. Then his eyes landed dead on mine. I could see the way his face tightened up. This man knew who I was, and he quietly whispered something to his sidekick, who in turn glanced in the saloon mirror.

As they both started to spread out from each other, I realized that I already had my two .44 revolvers in my hands. They were both raised towards the two bounty hunters, unseen under the table, with my kettle of coffee and full cup. The steam slowly rose from my cup and kettle, slightly blurring the view of the two men at the bar.

As soon as they started to turn around, I shot the first one that entered the saloon dead between the eyes, and the other in the gut so as not to kill him just yet. I wanted to get some information from the man before he died. I sat there sipping my coffee as he began to bleed out. Then, as I still sat at the table, I reloaded one revolver and then the other and stood up while slipping my irons back into their worn leather holsters. I slowly moved over to the dying man, while keeping an eye on the saloon doors just in case the town marshal had heard the gunfire.

"Why were you gunning for me?" I asked the bounty-hunter.

"Go to Hell, Creek!" the man exclaimed.

I took the toe of my boot and kicked him in the stomach, just above his gunshot wound as he let out a scream.

"You have a thousand dollar reward on your head," the bounty hunter cried. "Dead or alive. Your name is Ridge Creek, from South Texas. We figured it was you when we saw that fancy Mexican saddle on the stallion tied up out front."

I kicked him again but this time in the gut where he was shot.

He screamed even louder but continued, "You're wanted for the murder of a bunch of men, but it's said that you have killed just about every kind of living creature on this Earth. Women and children included. We were the first of the bounty hunters that found you, but you won't last Creek! If we didn't get you, somebody else will."

Now that I have heard what I wanted, I pulled my pistol out and whacked him across the head with it and said, "Let him bleed out. Maybe he will still be alive later so he can tell the others who are after me what happens to those that cross my path."

I reached down and went through the pockets of the dead bounty hunter and found a piece of folded paper.

When I opened it, the face of the man in the reflection at the waterhole looked back at me. You can't mistake those eyes. It stated that Captain Ridge Creek, ex-Texas Ranger, is wanted for the murder of a number of Texans and two officers of the law. That and the fact he had a one thousand dollar reward on his head, dead or alive. Signed by the Texas, State Governor.

That cleared up the question of what I am going to do. I'm going to stay alive any way I have to.

CHAPTER 20:

LAREDO, TEXAS

Rowdy Bates sat down on the white chair on the porch of the Lone Star Saloon. Pushing it back till it leaned up against the building nice and solid. Then the Texas Ranger Captain fished around in his shirt pocket until he extracted a cheap cheroot with a bright green string around it and a wooden match. He ran the tip of the match down the leg of his britches, and it sparked to life with a smell of sulfur. A bright blue and yellow flame burned as Rowdy Bates held the fire before his eyes for a moment deep in thought. Finally moving the end of the flame to the tip of his cigar until he puffed copious amounts of blue smoke.

Pondering on all the things that had happened in these last months. Who in the world would have ever thought that Captain Ridge Creek would be on the run for murder? As he sat there on the porch Marshal Deeds looked his way from across the street.

"Damn, every time that Marshal shows up he has some bad news," Rowdy said to Sergeant Travis Picket.

As soon as Deeds saw the new Texas Ranger Captain he made a beeline for the officer. Kicking up dust as he moved towards the Rangers at a desperate pace. The man held a folded up piece of paper in his hands.

"Howdy Marshal," Rowdy offered a greeting. "What's wrong now? I know something is up as every time you see me and rush over my way it is because you have a problem or some bad news."

"I bet-cha you ain't seen this," he said as he held up the folded piece of paper.

Rowdy stretched out his hand for the Marshal to give him more bad news. Ain't things already screwed up enough, the new Captain thought? The Marshal put the yellowish folded flier into his hand, and he slowly opened it as he pushed his chair forward until all four feet rested on the pine-plank floor.

"Son of a bitch," Rowdy said almost in a whisper.

"What is it, Captain?" Travis Picket asked.

Rowdy drew back his lips from his teeth and spat into the dusty street. Shaking his head from side to side at the current state of events. Then he passed the document to the Sergeant.

Travis opened the paper and read, "Ex-Texas Ranger Captain Ridge Creek. Wanted for the murder of Pedro Mendez, a couple of lawmen and the burning of Ragged Ridge Creek. There is a one thousand dollar reward on his head. Lord have mercy, Rowdy. How in the world could something like this happen to Ridge? He ain't no outlaw."

"Of course he ain't no outlaw, you dunderhead. Captain Creek has just been framed for something that Pedro Mendez worked up, for sure. Now that the old Mexican Rancher is dead there is no way to prove it right or wrong. So Ridge is on the run. He always told me that you just never know what is just around the corner when you venture out into the wild country. I guess Ridge has met his fate."

"I don't believe it for a minute," Travis retorted, all riled up. "First of all the Captain ain't a murderer. Yeah, he's a mite hard with outlaws and such sorts, but he never killed an innocent man on my watch nor your watch either. It was Ridge that kept us from all losing our scalps I don't know how many times."

"I reckon I can't believe it any more than you, Pard," Rowdy replied. "But you know how the law works just as well as I do. Things ain't always seen the same here up close as they are back somewhere like Austin or even in Washington. The farther away a decision is made, the farther from right it seems to be."

"Well, what are we going to do about it?" Travis asked. "We can't just let this happen to

Ridge. What if they kill him too? They already killed Toby, Weston and the boys. Of our old bunch there's only Clinton Westwood back at the El Paso Ranger post, and I heard that old Bill Vents had stayed on at Ridge's new ranch. I heard tell that the Captain up and gave the ranch to Bill and rode off for the Indian Territories."

"Well, we best send a telegram to Clinton and have him ride along with the next bull-whacker wagon train that heads this way," Captain Bates replied. "It ain't safe to travel alone. And I don't guess Bill Vents will want to carry on as a Ranger, him being so old and all. He had taken a mighty strong liking to the ranch life on Windy Ridge. Bill Hickok must have already heard about all this as I was told he stayed on for a spell in El Paso to play poker. It usually takes him a few weeks to lose all his money."

"There must be something we can do," Travis insisted. "I don't feel right just sitting by and doing nothing."

"I reckon we could take a few boys and head down to Eagles Pass and ask Judge Roy Bean what can be done," Rowdy replied. "He's an old friend of Ridge's, so at the very least he will let us know where the Captain stands. I ain't been there yet, but they say he built a saloon not far from the trading post that Rick Pawless owns. I wonder what happened to Tuc and Potak. Marshal Deeds said the old Judge is holding court there just like he did back in New Mexico before he was run off and here in the Laredo.

Not a week had passed when Captain Bates rode into the village of Eagles Pass. Old Rick's Trading Post stood there just like always, but a new building was built only a few hundred yards away from the small town up on a hill. It was called the Jersey Lilly Saloon. There was another sign that hung on the outside of the building that stated, "Judge Roy Bean Presiding."

Rowdy, Travis and another half dozen Rangers pulled up to the hitching rail of the Eagles Pass Trading Post.

"You boys stay here while Travis and I go see the old Judge" Rowdy ordered. "Rick's wife makes some mighty fine grub, so you boys go ahead and get something to eat. We'll be along shortly."

Judge Roy Bean

They rode up the bluff and to the front of the saloon just as the old Judge walked out onto the porch.

"I was wondering when you would make it out here to see me, Sergeant Bates," the old Judge said.

"It's Captain Bates now, Judge," Travis Picket corrected him.

But the old Judge just waved his hand in dismissal of what Travis had said. You could clearly see how the old man had aged and appeared to be suffering from poor eyesight along with now being well on the heavy side.

"I know why you come here, Rowdy," the old Judge said before the new Captain could get a word out. "There is a whirlwind out there, and if you are unlucky enough to step into it, you are in for the fight for your life on getting back out again. There ain't a damned thing you can do for Ridge now. He will have to see if he can get out of this one all on his own. When a man steps into that grey area of the law, he can expect the worst at times."

(End of Sundog Series 10)

TEXAS RANGER CREEK IN FULL CIRCLE

A note from the Author to the readers:

The next book to read after this series is Ragged Ridge Creek. The first book of the Ridge Creek Trilogy, Plus One. If you have already read those four books, then this book concludes the life and times of Texas Ranger Captain Ridge Creek and the final installment of the Sundog Series.

When I wrote the first book of the series, Ragged Ridge Creek I only intended to write a three book trilogy. When I saw I could not finish the story I was telling without writing another book I added on the Ridge Creek Trilogy, Plus One. That book was Lonesome Canyon. This I intended to be my last Western, or at least the last of Ridge Creek.

But the man wouldn't die. He was still alive in my mind, so I went back to his youth when he was just thirteen-years-old. And told the story, how I saw it in my imagination. How I saw the life of Ridge Creek.

Those of you that have read the two series, I thank you immensely. And I can only hope that you enjoyed reading them as much as I enjoyed telling these campfire tales.

For those of you that are just discovering Captain Ridge Creek, I genuinely hope you enjoy the story and the way in which I have told it.

TEXAS RANGER CREEK IN FULL CIRCLE

THE BOUNTY HUNTERS SERIES

Bounty Hunters - Rancor Maleficent #1

Bounty Hunters – Roberto Rodriguez #2

Bounty Hunters – Mister Tom Horn #3

Bounty Hunters – Marshal Hoss Cole #4

THE SUNDOG SERIES

Sundog Comanche #1

Sundog Daze #2

West to Ranger Creek #3

Ranger Creek and the Gunslinger #4

Texas Ranger Creek's Old West Adventures #5

Texas Ranger Creek – West to Tombstone #6

Texas Ranger Creek & Tombstone's Bloody Bucket #7

Texas Ranger Creek & Cowboy Justice #8

Texas Ranger Creek in Range War #9

Texas Ranger Creek and Full Circle #10

RIDGE CREEK TRILOGY + ONE

Ragged Ridge Creek #1

The Battle of Lost Valley #2

Chisholm Trail to Deadwood #3

Lonesome Canyon #4

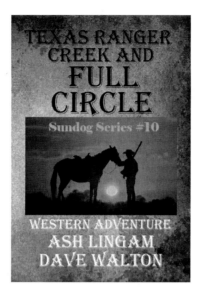

This is the tenth and last book of the Sundog Series and the life and times of Texas Ranger Captain Ridge Creek. Señor Pedro Mendez is one of the biggest cattle rustlers in all of Texas. A man with a foot in each country, stealing Texan cattle and selling them right back to the men he rustled them from. As Captain Ridge Creek's attention is turned from the Bogardus clan and towards the Mendez outlaw gang a personal conflict forms between the two men. Meanwhile, Ridge Creek is smitten by one Lola Zapata and considers a new life away from the violence. And Sergeant Bill Vents ponders his age and all his years as a Texas Ranger. Last but not least Captain Creek has sent the word to the Outlaw Lopez that he is on the hunt to kill him. An action-packed final installment of the Sundog Series will keep you entertained from cover to cover.

Captain Creek and his Texas Rangers stop the ranch baron Seth Bogardus from killing off the local cow-hands in the El Paso area. Only to find that his father, Lord Bogardus is on his way from Scotland to make amends for his son's lack of success in taking over every ranch with water rights from El Paso to the border with New Mexico sailing in his personal ship from Glasgow to Galveston. And on to cross the width of Texas with a wagon-train unlike any seen on the San Antonio trail. Hurricanes, shoot-outs, Comanche War Parties and captured hostages are all part of this ninth book of the Sundog Series. An Old West Tale of gunslingers and outlaws.

Marshal Rusty "Hoss" Cole was the law of Middletown County, California. Joining up with the bounty hunters, Rancor Maleficent and Roberto Rodriguez. Along with ex-Texas Ranger Rowdy Bates, Sheriff Biff Bain of Mayweather and a scribbler from the Chicago Evening Post, as the men make their way across Nevada, Utah, and Wyoming to attend the hanging of the infamous Tom Horn. Their destination was the Wild West town of Cheyenne. Train robberies, stray Comanche, Vigilante parties, and lost Cheyenne Braves are all a part of this Western Adventure. Taking a Federal Marshal across the line between the bounty hunter and the lawman, where the difference between the legal and the illegal is a fine gray line in the dust. Often not clearly visible, allowing for a man to inadvertently stray to the other side of the law without even noticing it. An original Old West Tale.

(Gunslinger Series No. 4)

Texan born Tom Horn was a notorious bounty hunter during the decades in the closing scene of the nineteenth century and the Old West. A man considered by many to be a hero and others an assassin. An Army scout who lived from this cash for flesh enterprise. Learning his skills of tracking and speaking the native languages from the Apache tribes. Then him using this same knowledge to kill those very people who taught him. As he worked farther west and into California Horn encountered his old enemies, Rancor Maleficent and Marshal Hoss Cole. The ever-humorous Roberto Rodriguez brings this unlikely crew together to make a final strike against the violent outlaws of the far West. Once again Ash Lingam gives us a vivid canvas like, description of the Old West and the characters who lived, fought and died there. The hardships and the humor with a dose of romance and a passel of lead and gun-smoke.

(Gunslinger Series #3)

Roberto Rodriguez continues to ride with the notorious Rancor Maleficent. Hunting down wanted men with money on their head. From Mayweather and Stockton to the Barbary Coast of San Francisco, these two soul snatchers continue to wreak violence on the outlaws of the west.

In this second episode of the Bounty Hunter gunslingers series, the dangerous duo hunt down such infamous outlaws as Black Bart, Buck English and the feared Boris the Butcher. A world where villains were many and the honest were few. Crossing paths with other famous bounty hunters of the time, such as Tom Horn and Isom Dart. The action is a-plenty and shoot-outs galore in the latest series by the Old West author Ash Lingam, racing to the top of the list of western writers of our times.

(Gunslinger Series #2)

Bounty Hunters were a part of the historical Old West. A profession that has been written about and depicted in novels and movies for decades. Ash Lingam's "Bounty Hunter Rancor Maleficent" is the first book in the Gunslinger Series, written in a style influenced by Sergio Leone and the spaghetti western films of the period.

Rancor Maleficent is one of these men. Trading dollars for bodies as he hunts men down for their reward. Assisted by Roberto, the duo of man-hunters travel the California Territories in the late 1800's, taking the law into their own hands. Hunting down men of reckless blood for a living. Rancor, already a legend due to his violent nature, with his humor afflicted accomplice, Roberto Rodriguez, in their quest to trade flesh for cash. Like most bounty hunters, looking for an easy way to make a living even if it involves risking their lives in exchange. Or perhaps it is the very nature of the profession that attracts recklessly bold men. The two men are on the hunt for three ex-sheriffs, a four fingered outlaw and an ex-Texas Ranger. Men who had strayed across the fine gray line between the law and the outlaw. Action, humor, and a good dose if led makes this new series one of Lingams best.

(Gunslinger Series #1)

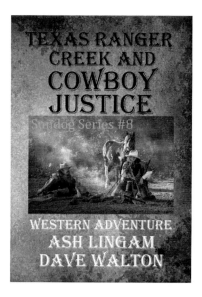

As the small Texas Ranger patrol returned from Tombstone, Arizona and New Mexico they ran across two dead cowboys out on the trail of the Great Plains to El Paso. They were murdered by bushwhackers with a badge. In an attempt to stop a deadly range war with the Scottish born Seth Bogardus, Texas Ranger Captain Ridge Creek brings his best Rangers from Laredo to face off with the infamous Marshal Dan Dowd, along with twenty hired gunslingers in beige dusters and Winchesters repeater rifles, guns for hire to the highest bidder.

Mister Bogardus himself, a wealthy ranch baron and the man with the intention of taking every substantial water source from the New Mexican border to the city of El Paso by force with the bounty hunter, Tom Horn at his side. The danger in Texas has not diminished, making the need for such men as Captain Creek and his band of Texas Rangers imperative. It is said, in order to kill wicked men you need a bad man, and Creek is up to the task. Ash Lingam reaches new heights with his latest novel of the Wild West and the Texas Rangers. Bringing the 1860s to life in his Tales of Western Adventures in Cowboy Justice.

(Sundog Series Vol. No. 8)

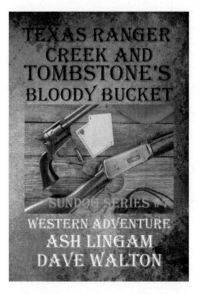

Texas Ranger Captain Creek leaves Mountain Man Seth Kinman, and heads for Tombstone, Arizona with Wild Bill Hickok to save a damsel in distress. The stealing of women and children is rampant by the Apache in the Arizona Territories. A complete lack of law west of El Paso leaving Creek, Hickok and his Rangers to sort out the mystery of who kidnapped Marta Enriquez. The hanging of Scorpion Jack and on to the gold mines of New Mexico. Creek, and his Rangers now on the chase of gunmen from a range war. Gunslingers, hostiles, romance, humor, hangings and a good dose of lead. Making legends of these Texas Rangers and Captain Creek as they come to life in his tales of adventure in the Old West.

(Sundog Series Vol. 7)

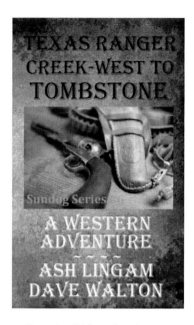

Texas Ranger Captain Ridge Creek continues to combat the Violence prevalent in the Texan territory after the Great Civil War. Along the trail, Creek meets Mountain Man Seth Kinman. Tracked by a Comanche War Party, hell-bent on killing the old Buffalo Hunter. From Laredo to Galveston, only to end up riding all the way across Texas, New Mexico and on to Tombstone to help out the Captain's old friend and gunfighter, James Butler Hickok. The state of Arizona is now fallen into a state of lawlessness, and Hickok has taken on himself to bring order to the area. Once again, Ash Lingam brings his characters to life mixing the historically factual and real-life Old West with his tales and the hardest lawman of all, Captain Creek or known to the Comanche as the feared "With Dead Eyes."

(Sundog Series Vol. 6)

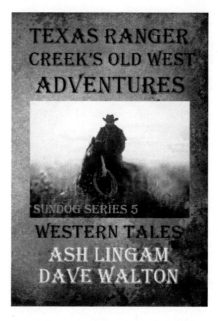

After surviving the battle of Kiowa Hill, Texas Ranger Captain Creek returns to Laredo to find the outlaw Bella Star is on the run and heading his way. Creek, his Texas Rangers, and Tonkawa Scouts are on her trail giving chase across the State of Texas to the New Mexican border. Run-ins with Comanche Warriors, Liberty Valdez, and the gunfighter James Butler Hickok among other famous Old West characters. The lawman Creek continues to fight to keep the Texan violence at bay. From gunslingers to Mountain Men, these are the Tales and Western Adventures of Captain Creek and his Rangers. The period is the decade of eighteen-sixty. The location, Texas. Hell is coming to breakfast!

(Sundog Series Vol. #5)

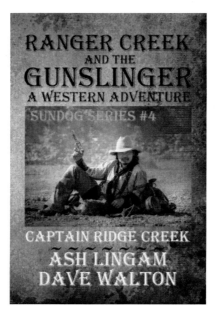

From Eagles pass with a knife fight to the death of two half Cherokee mountain men. To brief encounters with Lopez the Outlaw and his torturous ways. Ranger Creek of the Laredo Texas Rangers encounters the challenge of his lifetime in the face of staggering odds against Kiowa Warrior Braves on the trail to hell along the River Rio Grande. On to confront the well-known Texan Gunslinger King Fisher and his gang. Finally chasing the woman outlaw and stagecoach robber Bella Star, west across the Texan Badlands. Ash Lingam has created a true old style Western Lawman in the manner of such greats as Sergio Leone, Charles Portis, and Larry McMurtry with a taste of Quentin Tarrantino. A true Western Adventure.

(Sundog Series Vol. #4)

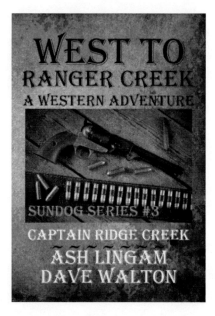

As Texas Ranger Captain Ridge Creek and his men survive a gunfight with Bob Lees Raiders in San Antonio, Texas the lawlessness in the state since the end of the Civil War has become rampant. It is eighteen sixty-six during the Reconstruction Period and many soldiers mustered out of the Armies, both North and South only to return to burned-out homes and long-gone families. Some turned to the trail West and Texan territory, bringing with them the hate and violence inherited from their four years of hell. Combined with the lack of military presence in Texas during these years of civil conflict the Comanche had gained a foothold and pushed the settlers back more than thirty miles as they continue their raiding parties unchecked across Texas and Mexico. With only the Texas Rangers to stand in their way. A historically factual novel with a peppering of famous Old West characters sprinkled in. Humor, tragedy, romance, bounty hunters, gunfighters and a strong dose of action make this third book of the Sundog Series a winner. Quite the Western Adventure.

(Sundog Series #3)

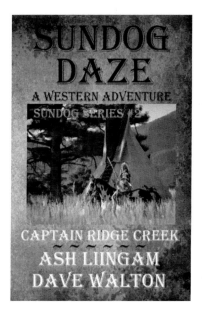

As the 1860's approach the lawlessness on the Texan border with Mexico was still rampant. Violent raids from banditos, outlaws, Comanche and Mexican gun hands hired by south of the border ranchers. It was an onerous task and the responsibility of the small band of Texas Rangers. Especially the Ranger the Comanche called With Dead Eyes. The man who instilled fear in the outlaws and Plains Indians alike. These were his younger years.

(Sundog Series Volume #2)

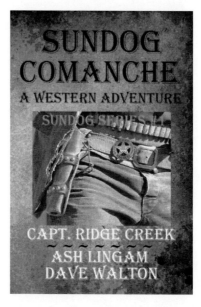

After the small pox plague killed off half the inhabitants of the small town of Ragged Ridge Creek, Texas the young Creek boy was orphaned. His father, Maxwell Creek provided him with his namesake of the town, Ridge. At thirteen taken onto work in the general store of an aging ex-gunfighter and lawman, Ridge Creek learned the tricks the trade. At sixteen he rides off to Austin to join the Texas Rangers. The rest is history.

(Sundog Series Volume #1)

As Captain Creek leaves Deadwood in the Dakota Territories and follows his fancy for the woman Cheyenne War Chief Pretty Nose, he heads westward into the Wyoming Territories, searching for the last of the great herds of buffalo. Hoping they will lead him to the ultimate point of his journey. To the Plains Indians and the big Cheyenne Village. Will Captain Creek's travels lead him to his fancy or to his own personal apocalypse? Every day the unexpected happens here in the Wild West of the Indian Territories.

(Ridge Creek Trilogy No. 4)

During the 1870's Ex-Texas Ranger and accused outlaw, Captain Creek is trapped and desperate and on the run from bounty hunters. He was framed by Pedro Mendez for slaughter and the burning of the town of Ragged Ridge Creek, in Southern Texas. As he finds a way to prove his innocence and in hopes to clear his name he meets up with his old partner, Wild Bill Hickok and a south of the border beauty, Blanca Flores. Rustlers, Mexican Bandits, Renegades, Outlaws, Kiowa Indians & Comanche.

(Ridge Creek Trilogy No. 1)

Major Creek of the Texas Rangers takes a patrol into the Indian Territories to meet up with Chief Quanah Parker. After the Sun Dance, calling the Comanche, Kiowa and Cheyenne warrior braves to attack buffalo hunters and white settlers making homesteads on their granted hunting grounds. A path that will, finally lead the Rangers to the Battle of Lost Valley. Leaving the Texas Rangers, Ridge hires on as a US Marshal and goes after the famous outlaw, John Wesley Hardin.

(Ridge Creek Trilogy No. 2)

During Ridge Creek's ride north, he and Nat Love traveled up the Chisholm Trail. Moving north towards the Dakota Territories, they saved a wagon train full of valuables from hostiles and then agree to help take the Wagon Train along with Martha (Calamity) Jane Canary to Deadwood, where Ridge takes a job as Deputy Sheriff under Sheriff Seth Bullock. His duties included riding shotgun on the Deadwood to Cheyenne stagecoach. The most dangerous stretch of land in the Black Hills.

(Ridge Creek Trilogy No. 3)

This is a story about a young surfboard and his travels to become a very special surfboard. When his new owner Kai and he learn to work magic. Following them in their travels with Mr. Volkswagen, their van, Sandy, Kai's girlfriend and Al, Sandy's Magic Surfboard.

Through the streets of Kathmandu. In the alleys of Old Delhi, to the mountains of Afghanistan, Pakistan and Nepal.   Across the dangerous deserts of Eastern Turkey, on to the beaches of Goa, India.   Places where many lived like pirates with adventurers, smugglers, hippies, and Monks.   Driving a Hippy Bus from Kathmandu to Amsterdam and return.

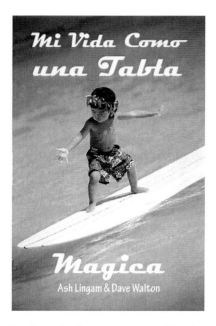

Este libro es sobre la vida de una Joven Tabla de Surf que se llama Style. Una tabla hecha por Mr. Greek quien le dio su alma y corazón. Y de su surfer Kai con quien se hace Soul Surfers. Y Style vuelve a ser su Tabla Mágica. También sobre los viajes que se hacen con el Mr. Volkswagen. Con su amiga, Sandy y su Tabla Mágica Al.

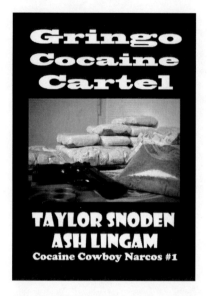

An inside true grit story of the Colombian, Peruvian and Bolivian underworld and several violent years before Pablo Escobar took charge of the cocaine narco trade. Escobar being far from the original of the heavy Cartel leaders during the seventies and early nine-teen eighties. There also existed a half dozen Gringo Cartels across South America. Mainly in Colombia and Bolivia. This is the story of one such gang and of the profits they gained and the terrible violence that they spread across two Continents. From their first flight in a mid-sized twin engine Cessna from the far away clandestine runways in Northern Colombia to the Bahamas with their first load of a thousand pounds of marijuana. Eventually the change to the far most lucrative business on the entire Continent. The Cocaine Trade. This is a story of a few high octane cocaine cowboys from Florida who decided to take their chances to possibly gain the vast fortunes that their Colombian counterparts were enjoying the fruits of. It is about an unlikely group of Gringos who teamed up to be a smuggling force to be reckoned with across all of Europe and the Americas in the late 1970's and early 1980's. While the getting was still there for those that do not divagate from danger or the violence that draw men of reckless blood to such environments.

TORNADO - When the color of the sky turns a yellowish green while the birds and animals start to run for cover in their disquietude, already sensing what is soon to come. A peculiarly strange stillness comes over your surroundings. Then you begin to see the dark turgid funnel shaped clouds begin to drop from the thick black masses of storm cells above, seeking out fuel for their apocalyptic and inordinate power leaving little escape for those not prepared for the dystopia to come.

CAVE - When we venture deep into the dark unknown cracks and crevices of our Mother Earth exploring a new part of the world. Not the Seas or Oceans. Nor the mountains or jungles but another part of our unexplored world. The deep and dark places under the earth's surfaces. A sport for the impetuous. Leading to inordinately dangerous adventures for those that are not the weak at heart. Those of us that do not divagate from danger.

(Short Stories)

www.ashlingam.com

ashlingamwriter@gmail.com

Instagram: Ash Lingam

YouTube: Ash Lingam

Face Book: Ash Lingam

TEXAS RANGER CREEK IN FULL CIRCLE

Made in United States
North Haven, CT
04 May 2022

18881241R00181